Returning to Me

S.L. STERLING

About the Book

I always wondered where I went wrong in my life when it
came to love.
I was serious with my high school sweetheart, Noah, or so
I thought. I went to college, and he enlisted in the service.
We stayed in contact regularly and then...nothing. I always
felt that something happened, perhaps he met someone
overseas and didn't know how to tell me.
Regardless, I took my broken heart, finished school, and
took over the family business running the only Christmas
Tree Lot in Willow Valley. In keeping with tradition Potts
Family Tree Farm always picks a charity to work with for
the holiday season. This year, I've partnered with a local
charity to help the children of military families who lost a
parent in the line of duty, celebrate Christmas.
After our first meeting I came home and immediately
noticed a dirty, partially ripped bag sticking out of my
mailbox by the road. I grabbed it and tried to make out
what was written on it, but it was so dirty and worn, all I
could see was a portrait of Santa Clause staring back
at me.
It was a Christmas Card.
One I'd never gotten – from eleven years ago.
As I read it tears streamed down my face. Noah asked me
to marry him, and he'd been waiting for me to respond to

the card because he'd been on a mission. I never got the card, so I'd never responded.

All these years I thought he'd never tried to contact me, and his parents had never said a word. So, I did what any woman would do today, I sent him a Facebook message, telling him how I only just received his card today, almost eleven years after it had been sent.

Now I wait...

Returning to Me

Copyright © 2025 by S.L. Sterling

ISBN: 978-1-989566-80-0

Paperback ISBN: 978-1-998649-49-5

Editor: Brandi Aquino, Editing Done Write

Cover Design: Thunderstruck Cover Design

Mindi

September 2024

I could feel the change of weather in the air as I walked down the main street of Willow Valley headed for The Crispy Biscuit. I'd kept myself busy with the tree farm and the community center, but in my quiet time, my mind wouldn't settle.

I pulled the door open and walked into The Crispy Biscuit, the smell of pumpkin spice in the air.

"Morning," Tristan greeted with a smile.

"Morning. I'm not too late to grab a pumpkin scone, am I?" I questioned.

"Let me check. Looks like you are in luck. We have two left." He winked, grabbing one from the tray.

"Great, on second thought, I'll take them both. I've

been wanting one since I heard you guys were making them again this year. They always go fast."

"That they do. Did you want a coffee as well?"

"Of course." I smiled.

"Grab a seat and I'll bring them over." He smiled, turning to make another pot of coffee.

I made my way over to my favorite corner booth and slid inside, waving to Brooke as I got settled before pulling out the paperwork I'd brought with me. I had to plan some of our Christmas activities this year at the community center.

"Here you go," Tristan said, placing both my coffee and scone on the table.

"Thank you." I smiled.

"What are we working on today?" he questioned.

"Just some holiday plans."

"Yeah, I guess that time of year is already close, isn't it."

"Yes, it's sneaking up quick. I'm sure you guys are already planning."

"Brooke might be." Tristan winked just as Brooke came up behind him.

"What might I be doing?" she asked, resting her chin on his shoulder.

"Planning for the holidays."

"You know it. If I don't start, things won't get done."

"Exactly," I added, digging in my purse for my pen.

"Ah, look, Ethan and Peggy," Brooke said, waving in their direction as they walked through the front door.

I waved to them both, glad that they were here. Ethan had been one of the steadiest volunteers we had since he'd settled in Willow Valley, and both he and Peggy, along with his daughter Melinda, always helped with the Christmas dinner at the center. I was glad that I'd have their brains to pick, but one look at Ethan's face told me something wasn't right.

"Ethan, Peggy, how about you join me?" I called out, waving them over as they stepped inside.

Peggy placed her hand on Ethan's arm and whispered something before making her way over to where I was sitting. She slid into the seat across from me.

"I'll get you guys some coffee," Tristan said.

"Oh, and could we also each grab a couple of those wonderful pumpkin cookies."

"You know it," Brooke said, moving toward the counter to grab them.

"Morning," I greeted.

"Morning, Mindi," Peggy said, slipping her coat off her shoulders. "How's the tree lot coming along this year?"

"Good, the trees are healthy. I was just speaking with Connor Darling and Gabe Bentley. They are going to help me cut some trees for the fresh-cut lot, and I have already lined up a couple of kids from the school to help run the lot in December."

"Wonderful. I wonder if Ethan and I should come out and pick one for you to deliver."

"Sure, anytime, anytime. Just call me, and I'll take you out on the farm. It might be easier before the snow flies. You'll need one for the store as well, I take it?"

Peggy had been getting trees from me since she moved to Willow Valley, and the suggestion of coming to the farm normally would have made her smile, but not today. Today, her eyes looked heavy.

"Peggy, is everything okay?" I questioned, worried that perhaps something was wrong with her or Ethan.

"Haven't you heard?" she questioned, bringing her hand to her chest just as Ethan came over to the table with two cups of fresh coffee.

"No, what is it? Are you both okay?" I asked, looking up to see Ethan had the same somber look on his face.

"We are fine, but I'm surprised no one notified you," Ethan said, sitting down beside Peggy and removing his hat.

"Notified me about what?" I asked, a feeling of dread and worry building inside of me.

"Heidi and John Lancaster were both killed in an ambush last night."

Suddenly, my mouthful of pumpkin scone didn't taste

so good as I thought of poor little Sarah Lancaster, their daughter. She had been coming to the community center religiously, even after her parents were deployed. She stayed with Rick, Maggie, and their daughter Hilary whenever her parents were gone. Rick was deployed at the same time as Heidi, and John and I knew she had been having a hard time adjusting to her new normal but being with her friend Hilary made it a little easier for her. She and I had talked a lot recently; we'd become rather close over the years.

"Oh, dear me. I feel like I could be sick," I said, dropping the scone on the plate in front of me.

"I've been feeling the same since this morning when Ethan told me the news," Peggy said, looking at me. "Before they got news of the deployment, Heidi came into the shop and was beside herself. She worried about how her daughter was going to handle them being gone for the holidays, if it came to that. She was worried about how they'd give her a Christmas this year, being so far away. I'd planned on nominating them at the center for help, but I think now, given the circumstances, we all need to look after Sarah this year," Peggy said, dumping a packet of sugar into her coffee.

Each Christmas, the center helped those in need, providing dinner or gifts at Christmastime, sometimes both. I took nominations, and if I knew of someone that was already having trouble within the community, their names automatically went in. Unfortunately, this year, we'd always chosen our family.

"After Ethan got off the phone with one of the military sergeants, he called me and asked me to make some arrangements for flowers to be delivered to the funeral home."

"Do you need help with choosing flowers?" I questioned.

Ethan slipped into the booth with a tray of coffee and cookies.

"No, but Ethan said he found out from the sergeant that Heidi and John had nothing in place for Sarah. Neither of them had any family, which means..."

"Sarah will go into foster care," I muttered.

I wanted to cry thinking of Sarah and the fact that she'd not only lost her entire world but, if we couldn't find someone to look after her, she'd be ripped away from the only home she'd ever known. There weren't many eligible families in Willow Valley that could take in a child.

The door to the cafe opened, and in walked Trinity and Thomas. They immediately made their way over to the table.

"Everyone already hear?" Trinity asked.

"Sadly," I said.

"I think she should be the community focus this year." Trinity added, "In fact, I'll insist on it."

I softly smiled. Trinity had such a heart, as did Peggy. It didn't surprise me that they were so close.

"No worries, she already will be," I added. "Peggy was going to nominate her anyway, but considering the circumstances, there was no way I'd even consider another recommendation over this. We will just add her to the list of recipients."

"What will happen to her? Will she stay with Rick and Maggie?" Trinity questioned, looking over at Ethan.

"No, I'm afraid not. When I spoke to the sergeant this morning, he told me she'll be placed into foster care. However, it's going to take time to get things situated. So, she will probably move—"

"In with me," I said finishing his sentence, realizing that I'd been one of the few approved homes in the direct area, in case of an emergency such as this.

"Well, that is a blessing," Trinity said, smiling over at me.

"Sure is," Peggy added.

"I'm glad you think so."

Everyone looked at me, understanding on their face.

"Nah, Mindi, you'll do fine. You have all of us to help if need be," Ethan added, reaching across the table and patting my hand.

I couldn't help but smile as I fought back the tears that were threatening to fall.

A heavy sadness fell over everyone at the table, and

while Peggy and Trinity started talking amongst themselves, I sat there. First, thoughts of how Sarah must be feeling flooded my mind, and then a memory popped into my head I hadn't thought of in a while.

I'd just started volunteering at the center back in September 2015. I'd had a hard time all fall, and it seemed to get worse as we moved into the holiday season that year. Noah, my high school sweetheart, was over in Afghanistan on a peacekeeping mission while I was busy over here, helping the less fortunate. I'd spent the entire season volunteering my time because, in a way, it had made me feel closer to Noah.

I'd written to him just after I finished dealing with a girl about my age who'd lost her new husband when his vehicle hit a landmine. It had been the most challenging thing I'd ever had to deal with at the center and hit me in a way it probably shouldn't have. Much like the news from today had.

I wrapped my hands around my coffee, shoved thoughts of that Christmas out of my mind, and forced myself to focus on the conversation in front of me.

Mindi

Mid - November 2025
14 months later

"Morning, Mindi!"

I looked up as I stepped into The Crispy Biscuit to see Brooke breeze on by with a coffeepot in hand.

I couldn't help but smile. Brooke was always a cheerful burst of energy, especially at this time of year. "Morning."

"Grab a seat wherever you like, and I'll be there in a minute to take your order. Tristan and Melinda both have colds, so we are a little shorthanded this morning."

"Not a problem, Brooke. I just came to pick up the sandwiches and muffins for the luncheon over at the community center and to drop this off," I said, holding up the flyer Sarah and I had created for the tree farm.

"Ah yes, put that up on the community board and I'll be right with you. People have been asking me already when they will be able to come out and get their trees."

Every week for as long as I could remember, I'd been coming here to pick up food for the Friday luncheons. I'd been one of the first steady customers Brooke had after starting her bakery counter before then taking over the family business.

I glanced down at my watch, hoping that the items I'd ordered were ready to go. We had a large group coming in today. I'd worked so hard on this program for military families over the years, and it had become bigger than I'd ever imagined it would. We now had a set of steady volunteers who came to help young kids and spouses deal with the impact military life had on them.

On weekends, we had arts and crafts, along with game days, and every Saturday and Sunday, we either provided lunch or dinner for the children. Throughout the week we had coping groups for the spouses who had lost their significant others, or for those whose partners were deployed, and just recently we had put out a call for a counselor to help those children who had suffered the loss of a parent.

After everything I'd been through with Sarah in the

past year, I knew the community could benefit from having a counselor on staff. We still hadn't found someone, but something kept telling me we were getting close.

A chill ran through me as I stood waiting at the counter. I'd been feeling off for the past few days, and while I'd like to think it was the change of weather, I hoped I wasn't getting sick. It wouldn't surprise me, things had just felt off this year. I watched as Brooke flew from table to table and then came back over and placed the now empty coffeepot on the counter, turned, and smiled.

"How are things going with Sarah?" she questioned, wiping her hands on her apron.

"Oh fine. She still hasn't been overly talkative, which has me worried, but we are making do. It has only been a little over a year since she lost her parents. I just dropped her over at Bluebird Books for the reading program and to spend some time with Gracie. Since Hilary and her parents moved she has been glued to Gracie."

"Well, hopefully that will help some. Any luck in finding a counselor yet?"

"Sadly, no, not even any calls regarding the position, which has me worried."

"Well, don't give up. I'm sure someone will contact you soon."

"I sure hope so."

"Any word on placement for Sarah?"

I shook my head. "I just spoke with the military rep last night. She advised me they don't feel comfortable moving Sarah to the adoption center yet. They want her to stay in a stable environment until the holidays are over, so she will stay with me until after Christmas."

"Might be better that way."

"I agree. Oh, is my order ready?"

"Mindi, as you can see, I've been swamped this morning. Do you think you could come back in half an hour? I have the guys working on them right now. They are just finishing them up."

I smiled, knowing just how busy she always was at this time of the year.

"No problem. How about you put one of your award-winning cinnamon buns on a plate along with a cup of coffee and I'll just grab a table and wait?" I winked. "I also wanted to talk to you about booking some desserts and food for the Christmas dinner at the center as well."

"That I can do, and yes, if I get your order in now, I'll be able to make my holiday plan and not overbook myself."

"No problem. Looks like you may have to hire more hands soon."

"That and put in an expansion. I'm afraid we are quickly outgrowing this place," Brooke said as she served up a cinnamon bun and poured me a cup of coffee.

"Extra hands should help. No need to move from this place. Willow Valley wouldn't be the same without you in this location. My parents used to come here when your parents ran the place." I winked as I grabbed the cinnamon bun, while Brooke carried over my cup of coffee to one of the few free tables left. She set the mug down on the table and then grabbed one of her order forms and a pen.

"If you can get this back to me within the next week, I'd appreciate it."

"No problem. Thank you," I said, smiling as she took off to the kitchen.

I was exhausted. I'd run on adrenaline most of the day. Iris had brought Sarah over to the center for lunch and crafts, and now we were on our way back to the farm. My body ached and was craving the warmth of a hot bath, a cup of tea, and perhaps a holiday movie to help lift my spirits.

It had been another emotionally draining day. I seemed to be having more of those lately, knowing that the closer we got to December, the closer I was to my time with Sarah ending. I'd never been more thankful to have Ethan, Peggy, Trinity and Thomas along with a couple of other retired military members there to help with every-thing else that was going on.

Peggy and Trinity arrived after their hired help showed up at the bookstore and flower shop. After afternoon crafts had begun, we grabbed a coffee and discussed putting out another request for a counselor, which was on the top of my list to work on in the coming week.

"What did you want for supper?" I asked Sarah as I turned onto the road we lived on.

"I'm not that hungry." She sighed and then pointed at the mailbox at the end of the driveway. "There is mail," she muttered.

I stopped at the end of my driveway and glanced at the old red mailbox my father had put up all those years ago. The flag was up, notifying me I had mail. I debated just getting it tomorrow but noticed a clear bag sticking out of the closed door. Our neighbors occasionally left us food in the mailbox in a plastic bag, and while the bears should be in hibernation by now, it didn't feel right leaving it.

I let out a sigh and shoved open the car door and quickly opened the mailbox. Instead of food, all that sat there were a few envelopes and the clear plastic bag with a large sticker on it that read lost mail, so with little thought, I grabbed the pile and climbed back in the car and handed it to Sarah.

Once we were inside, Sarah took off to her room, and I

took a hot shower, then I heated the leftover soup in the fridge, made us both some toast and some tea, and made my way into the living room with a tray. We found a movie on TV watching it while we ate together.

When the credits rolled, I glanced over at Sarah, who was lying on the couch with her eyes closed.

"Ready for bed, sweetheart?" I questioned, rubbing her leg.

"I can barely keep my eyes open," she muttered as we both got up and I followed her to her room.

She crawled into bed and pulled the covers over her.

"No worries; it's been a long day. Good night, sweetie," I whispered, placing a kiss on her forehead, and then shut the overhead light off.

"Night."

I stood in the doorway and watched her as she snuggled up with her favorite teddy bear, then I turned the nightlight on and pulled the door partially closed.

I made my way back to the living room and cleaned up the dishes from supper. I'd just placed everything in the dishwasher when I looked at the pile of mail Sarah had put on the counter. After I'd wiped down all the counters, I was about to head back into the living room but stopped. Frowning, I made my way over and picked up the plastic bag, examining the contents.

Finally, curiosity got the best of me. I'd never received

one of these bags before, but I knew that when the post office lost a letter and finally found it, this was how they sent it. Upon closer inspection I noticed that dirt coated the bag, making it look as though someone had dragged it through a mud puddle. How long had this been lost, I wondered.

"What on earth is it?" I wondered aloud to myself, grabbing my craft scissors and cutting the top of the bag open. I carried it into the living room and emptied the contents onto my lap. A faded green envelope sat on my lap, and while I tried to make out whose name was on the envelope, it proved to be difficult. It too was dirty, and aside from the "Min" that was written on the front, the entire last name had rubbed off, along with most of the address.

I shook my head and carefully opened the torn envelope, pulling at the contents inside. It was a card, and when I flipped it over, a Santa Claus in pink camouflage stared back at me.

I frowned as I opened the card to see handwriting I'd have known anywhere but hadn't seen in years. I swallowed hard as I glanced at the date on the card: Christmas 2015. This couldn't be possible; it had taken ten years to get to me...

I frowned as I read the words written inside, then tears flooded my eyes and began rolling down my cheeks. Ten years later, I'd finally gotten a response from the letter I'd sent him all those years ago. My stomach flipped and then sank as I read the words, and I immediately knew the answer to why I'd never heard from him.

Noah had asked me to marry him, and I'd never responded.

Noah

"Thanks so much for everything, Clay. You as well, Iris," I said, holding my hand out. "You really did help me feel back at home."

"No problem, Noah. We were happy to have you stay with us, and if the house isn't ready yet, know that your room is still available for a couple more nights," Iris added.

I'd been staying at the bed-and-breakfast since I'd returned to town, but today I'd finally gotten the keys to my new place.

"Well, it's nice to know I have a place should I need it." I smiled as I placed my bag in my truck.

"Of course, anytime, and if you need any help to get things from the storage area, just let me know. Iris can always take care of things here with my mother for a couple of days," Clay said, placing his arm around her and pulling her into him.

I'd forgotten what a close-knit community Willow Valley was, and it was almost surreal being back here after all these years. The last time I'd been here was to bury my mother; the next was to put my father in the old-age home where he was now living. Dementia had set in only nine months ago, and when I went out to visit him last week, he no longer knew who I was.

"Thanks, I might just take you up on that," I said, holding my hand out toward Clay.

We shook hands, then I hugged Iris before climbing into my truck. Starting the engine, I backed out of the driveway, waved goodbye, and headed toward the small grocery store.

Twenty minutes later, I wandered through the aisles that hadn't really changed since before I'd left. I loaded some things into my cart and then made my way to the cashier.

Placing the items I'd picked up on the belt, I waited my turn while the cashier dealt with a woman ahead of me. As I waited, I noticed a flyer from the community center; they were looking for help for the holidays.

"Can you tell me what the Holiday Elves are about?" I asked the cashier, pointing at the card.

"Oh, sure can. I volunteer there on my days off. It's a charity that helps aid young children in the community.

They are mostly children of military families whose parent or parents are on active duty. It gives them a place to go, to be with other kids in the same situation, so they don't feel so alone. From now until after Christmas, we have game days, and we do special lunches on the weekends for the kids, as well as Thanksgiving dinner and Christmas dinner. It's a fantastic program, and it's rewarding."

"Sounds like it would be something that I might be interested in helping with," I said, taking a picture of the flyer with the information.

"You're new to the area? I've not seen you around here before."

I chuckled. "Yes, sort of. I grew up here, so not really new to the area. I've been staying over at the bed-and-breakfast but finally got the keys to my new place today."

"Oh, well, in that case, welcome back. What do you do for work?" the young girl asked.

"Thanks. I spent most of my younger years serving in the military, but now I'm a counselor who specializes in working with vets and children."

I looked back down at the paper and read it over again. This was how small towns worked, everyone was always curious about the new person.

"Well, if you are seriously looking for something to do, the holiday elves are a wonderful way to give back. They also add to the program at Christmas. The entire community does a fundraiser for the less fortunate in the community, and I've heard through the grapevine, which is rather small in this town, that this year we are focusing on the young girl who lost her parents in an ambush during a peacekeeping mission last year. She was only eleven at the time, and an only child. She has been staying with the woman who runs the community center but will be sent to foster care soon."

I nodded, realizing that I was one of the lucky ones who made it out when I knew many people didn't. Hell, one of my best friends was one of the unfortunate ones and had gotten killed right in front of me.

"You think it might be something you are interested in? I know the organizer personally and would be happy to introduce you. They have also announced they were looking for a counselor just recently. I'm sure they'd be happy to speak with you."

I thought for a moment. I didn't really have permanent employment at the moment and had no clue what sort of opportunities there might be out here. The only postings I'd seen had been in surrounding areas, nothing right in Willow Valley.

"I could even give you Ethan's number. He is another retired military man who helps at the center."

"Thank you, but there is no need. I think I'll call them once I get settled, or perhaps I'll just drop in," I said and smiled.

She gave me a small smile and continued packing up the few things I'd gotten.

"Have a good night," I said once I paid for my order and grabbed my bags of groceries.

"You too, and welcome back to Willow Valley. I hope to see you around!" she yelled as I made my way toward the exit. I loaded my things into the back of my car and then climbed into the driver's seat and fired up the engine, only to see a flyer on my windshield. I quickly reached for it, removing it and bringing it into the car.

Memories flooded me the moment I looked down at the flyer for Potts Tree Farm. I'd often wondered over the years what had happened to the farm. Did Mindi's parents still own it? Was she still in town somewhere? My parents had become tight-lipped about her and her family after they found out I never got an answer to my proposal. A few months later, my parents left Willow Valley, returning a few years later after my father retired. I never heard of Mindi or the Potts family again. The last information I'd gotten was from the letter I'd gotten from Mindi, the year her father had finally turned the tree farm into a business. I never got a response to the letter I'd sent answering that letter of hers, and I'd never heard from her about the proposal.

I often wondered if she'd gotten involved with someone else while I'd been gone and just hadn't had the heart to tell me. It wasn't uncommon for that to happen;

hell, I'd watched it happen to at least three of the guys in my platoon the year after I'd sent the card. Seeing their pain sort of made me happy that I had heard nothing; however, as time passed, the not knowing seemed to be worse in ways.

I felt broken for a long time, but then I focused my sights on my career and decided the military was where I was staying. It became easier. Soon, the only family I had was my military family, but three tours later, being away from home and having a normal life began calling to me. When it came time to re-enlist, I decided I'd had enough. I wanted a life that didn't involve hurting others, plus I had been dealing with some major PTSD symptoms that were making my job harder and some days my life impossible.

So, I took a leave before I resigned and got the help I needed, then started taking some classes and, while still employed by the military, I studied and became a counselor to help others with PTSD. I still worked for the military on a very part-time basis, but was craving something a little different, and this might be the thing I was looking for.

The steady beeping of the microwave caught my attention, and I opened the door, removing the microwave dinner I'd grabbed for tonight. I placed it on a plate and carried it and the bottle of beer I'd just opened into the living room.

I'd barely unpacked anything, and I had more space than I knew what to do with after all those years of sharing a bunk with my brothers. I'd, however, hooked up the TV. I sat down in my new chair and flipped through the channels, finding a hockey game to watch for the night, and dug into my dinner.

Once finished, I grabbed the napkin that sat beside my plate and wiped my mouth, then looked down to see the card I'd removed from my windshield. On it was the same stand Mindi had sent me a picture of all those years ago. The paint was faded now, but I could still read the words, and as I read over the flyer, my mind instantly went to thoughts of her.

I grabbed my phone and opened a new browser. I was probably asking for trouble as I began typing her name into it. I was about to hit send, but stopped. What was I doing? Had I forgotten what it was like trying to get over her? Obviously, I had. Nothing good could come from looking her up, so I put my phone down and went back to watching the hockey game.

The moment the game was over, I found myself back online. Friends from the military who'd left at the same time I had were bugging me to get set up on social media, so I went to Facebook and created a profile, then looked them up, sending a friend request to each of them.

They'd also been on me to get into the dating scene. I'd given that some thought and quickly decided that the online dating scene really wasn't for me. I'd prefer to meet someone in person and get to know them slowly, but I was carrying a lot of baggage from being in the military. While I'd worked through a lot of them, I still had wounds.

I was also dealing with the wounds of being back here in Willow Valley, dealing with my father, and all the thoughts and memories of Mindi I'd pushed to the side and not really dealt with.

I had to know what she'd been up to. I'd planned on driving out to her parents' place when I left the inn tonight but decided against it. I wasn't sure I was ready to find out the truth just yet, even though it was killing me inside, but now that I knew the tree farm was still here, I had to know if she was too.

As I sat there, I typed her name into the search bar on Facebook and hit enter, hoping her name was still the same. Seconds later, her picture appeared before me.

I took my time, slowly scrolling through her profile, looking at the pictures she'd posted. It appeared from this anyway that she was still single, perhaps never married, and from the looks of it, she didn't have children. My vision blurred as I continued scrolling, and I wiped at my eyes, blinking a few times. What had she been doing all this time if she wasn't married? What would have happened to us had she accepted my proposal? Would we have a house full of kids? Would we still be together?

All the questions I knew I needed answers to floated through my mind. It was the only way I'd be able to move on with my life and start a relationship with someone new. I also knew there would only be one way to find out. I just needed to find the courage to actually take the steps to ask them.

Mindi

"Do you think that you'll be able to get the trees cut before the weekend?" I asked Connor and Gabe as we made our way to the front of the house.

On their way back from Cedar Landing to pick up farm supplies, they'd stopped by to find out what section of trees I wanted cut for the pre-cut lot.

"I don't see it being a problem," Gabe answered, looking to Connor for his input.

"Should be good as well. There are a few more things to get done around the ranch to get ready for winter, but the help can take care of most of it, freeing up my time," he added. "Perhaps I'll bring Cadence with me and she can pick out a tree that day."

"Let me know. I'll have a few others marked by then—

two for Brooke, and two each for Trinity and Peggy, and one for Clay and Iris over at the bed-and-breakfast."

"You just let us know what to cut, and it will be done," Gabe said, winking at me.

"I'll send a farmhand over to deliver them to town for you as well," Connor added.

"Same here," Gabe agreed.

"You guys are too good to me," I said, thankful for their help.

"Not a problem, Mindi. Hopefully, we can get your dad's old truck up and running next year, and then you'll be able to do the deliveries, or at least hire someone to do them."

I looked over at the old truck. I remembered when Dad bought it. He'd had his first successful year running the tree lot and invested back into it, getting a large enough truck to deliver trees to town, so it made it easier for some of the older people in the community. It had served him and I well throughout the years, but last year it had broken down on me just before the holiday season. I'd not had the time or the funds to have it repaired, so Gabe and Connor helped me get it into the barn, and I'd been saving for the repairs since.

"It would be nice to revive the old Potts Tree Farm truck." I smiled, looking at the paint. It would need touching up.

"We'll get it done," Gabe said, heading toward his truck, Connor following.

I waved to each of them and then headed inside out of the cold, damp weather. After I ate and made a hot cup of tea, I made my way over to the couch with my laptop. I had a bunch of work to do for the community center, so I opened my laptop and got to work on the food order. As I picked up my notepad to make some notes, I heard something hit the floor. I made my note quickly and, with a sigh, looked down at my feet to see that pink camouflage Santa staring up at me. I forgot I'd tucked it into my notepad last night.

"What is that?" I heard Sarah ask behind me, then she came over and picked the card up off the floor, looking at it before handing it to me.

I looked down at the old worn card in my hand and let out a sigh before opening it up and reading it again. It was like I was torturing myself.

"This was in the bag that was delivered yesterday," I muttered, letting out a sigh as memories of Noah immediately ran through my mind as I read what he'd written all those years ago, and as I stared at his words, guilt and regret filled me.

Regret because I never should have said I wanted to wait to marry him until he returned after we'd gotten news of his deployment. Guilt because I couldn't imagine how he must have felt when I never responded through no fault of my own. It's just I knew he'd been struggling with being away from home, and I could only imagine how he must have felt after I never answered him.

"It looks like a Christmas card."

I sat there staring at the card, thinking back to that Christmas.

"That's exactly what it is," I said, closing it back up.

"Do you know who it's from?"

"I do."

"Who? It's odd that a holiday card gets lost, isn't it?"

"It is odd that it got lost. It is from someone who I used to be very close to."

"What happened to them?"

I remembered going to the bus station the night I knew he was supposed to come home on leave in January. I waited long after the last bus had left for him, but he never appeared. I attempted to speak with the sergeant on duty, but they refused me any information, just saying he wasn't on the list to come home. That night, after leaving a message with his parents, I immediately went home and wrote a letter to him. In fact, I wrote every week for the entire year and never got a response from him.

I had checked the mail every day with the same result. My mind began playing horrible tricks on me after a while. I'd think I saw him across the street, waiting outside the community center where I volunteered, and in various other places around town. Then came the day I was certain he must be dead, just like the young girl's husband I'd helped at the center. The easiest choice for me was to accept that he'd been handed that horrible fate. No letters, not a word from him, and while I mourned him, I never truly let him go.

His parents, who had always remained distant from the community, continued that pattern. They refused to talk to me on the phone or in person, and then the following winter, shortly before Christmas, they moved out of town without a word to anyone. I found out only because my father had gone to deliver their tree and had found their house empty.

I spent most of that holiday season in tears, still searching for any word of Noah. Not that I hadn't spent most of the year doing that, but this time I searched everywhere, including all funeral announcements from the past year, but there was nothing. It appeared he'd vanished off the face of the earth just like his parents. I'd even reached out to the military again, but they refused to provide me any information since I wasn't a relative or his spouse.

A couple of years later, Noah's parents returned to Willow Valley, and just like before, they kept to themselves. I, of course, had moved on, but every Christmas, memories of Noah haunted me—and still did.

Now, as I sat staring at this card, I knew I was wrong. It wasn't a wonder his mother gave me the cold shoulder. I could only imagine what Noah had said to them, or perhaps he had said nothing and just told them he had never heard from me.

As time passed, I'd moved into a wonderful relationship with a man who lived on the outskirts of Willow Valley. As the years passed, that relationship fell apart, and then both my parents fell ill, and I moved back home and took over the farm. I dated now and again, but never got involved in anything serious. In fact, the last date I'd gone on had been a disaster, and I'd vowed not to be set up again. Shortly after that, Sarah moved in.

Even though I'd never truly known what happened to Noah, each time I thought about him, it made me wonder if what my mind had conjured up to protect me had been true. There was some reason I'd never truly accepted the fact that he'd been taken from this world. It was as if my heart knew he was still out there somewhere.

"It's a complicated story," I said, placing the card inside my binder.

I looked over at her, at the sad look on her face.

"Did your friend die, like my mom and dad?"

I smiled softly while fighting back the tears I could feel burning. "To be honest, Sarah, I don't know."

"Well, if you don't know, then maybe you should try to find him," she said, shrugging.

"I wish it were that easy, sweetie. I tried to find him once, a long, long time ago, but was unsuccessful."

"Maybe you could try again. You never know. I mean, the card found you after all this time."

Perhaps I could reach out, I thought to myself. I knew many people in the military now, and many had settled right here in the area. Chances were that if Noah was still alive, someone would know of him.

"Maybe you are right. Maybe I'll try again."

"I think you should. Can I watch some TV?"

"Of course you can."

"Can Sparkles sit with me?"

I looked over to see Sparkles, my cat, lying across the couch, and nodded.

"You know, you've lived here for over a year, you do not need to ask. Sparkles loves sitting with you." I winked.

"Thanks," Sarah said, making her way to the couch where she sat down and pulled Sparkles into her lap while changing the channel to find something to watch.

I turned back to my computer and pulled up the browser and immediately thought of Ethan. Surely, he'd have crossed paths with him at some point or knew someone who had. I grabbed the phone and was about to dial Peggy and Ethan's number when I decided against it. I knew it would only lead to questions I wasn't sure I was prepared to answer.

Perhaps I could go about this differently, I thought. Maybe I could find him myself. I opened my Facebook profile and clicked on the search bar. I glanced over my shoulder to see Sarah focused on whatever show she was watching, and then I carefully typed his name into the search bar and moved the mouse so that the pointer hovered over the search button. I tapped the mouse, my stomach flipping at the thought of seeing him with another woman. I wasn't sure if I wanted to know if he found someone else, perhaps had a family. I picked up my mug and sipped my hot tea, then looked at the screen, my eyes falling to his name.

I was about to click on it when I stopped.

Perhaps all of this was better left where it belonged, which was in the past. Perhaps it was better to think of him as gone. Opening up a can of the past normally didn't have good consequences. Whatever our relationship was then, it was now in the past for a reason, right? Plus, I had a lot on my plate right now with the tree farm, Sarah, and community center. I didn't need to complicate things further, did I?

I listened to my gut and navigated away from the search page, opening up my email instead, content with my decision. I responded to a couple of emails, did some work on the holiday events, and then made dinner.

As the evening went on, I did my best to ignore that nagging voice in the back of my mind that kept coming forward, wondering about Noah. While Sarah continued to watch TV, I got up and made my way into the kitchen, pulled out the hot air popper, and made us some popcorn.

I grabbed two sodas from the fridge, my mind once again wandering to Noah.

While waiting for the popcorn to pop, I headed to my bedroom, changed into my pajamas, and opened my small closet. I turned the light on and looked up at the top shelf to see the old worn shoebox I'd shoved up there years ago. I reached up and grabbed it, carefully pulling it down, and carried it to the living room, then made my way back to the kitchen for the bowl of hot popcorn.

"What's in the shoebox?" Sarah asked as I carried in the popcorn and drinks.

"Letters," I said, handing her one bowl and a pop while I placed the other in front of me and grabbed each of us a blanket from the closet.

I sat down and pulled the old shoebox in front of me. It had been years since I'd thought of this box. Dust covered the top, but as soon as I lifted the lid, I smiled.

"Letters from whom?" Sarah questioned.

The entire bundle of letters from Noah was exactly as I'd left them. I'd kept every single one of them, starting from when he'd left Willow Valley to attend training camp, right through to the very last letter I'd received.

I shoved a couple of kernels of popcorn into my mouth as I pulled the brittle elastic off the bundle of envelopes and placed them down in front of me, just in time for Sparkles to crawl into my lap. I gently ran my hand over her head and listened as she purred.

"Letters from my friend Noah, the same person who sent me the card," I replied, picking up the envelope on top and opening it.

"He wrote all of those?" Sarah asked, peeking into the box.

"He did. Want to hear some of them?" I questioned.

Sarah adjusted the blanket on her lap and nodded, shoving some popcorn into her mouth.

"Okay, well, I hope you are ready for one hell of a story," I said as I pulled the first letter from the envelope.

"Got popcorn, a drink, a blanket. I think I am ready." She giggled, turning her attention to me.

Sarah shifted on the couch until she was comfortable and listened to me intently as I began reading the first letter in the pile. It took only a few words to transport me back, and soon my throat was tight and tears blurred my vision.

It was almost three in the morning when I finished. Sarah was sound asleep on the couch and had been for some time when I'd gotten to that last letter. My chest ached and my eyes hurt from crying as I recounted all the good times we'd shared—and some of the not-so-good times. I got up and grabbed the card that still sat on the table and opened it again, reading over his question. All I could think about was where we would be now had I gotten his card when I was supposed to.

Would we have married? Had children? Moved to

another part of the world? Would I have left Willow Valley? All these unanswered questions were driving me crazy. Yet they'd have to remain that way, I thought to myself. There was no way I would ever know the answers to them, I thought to myself as I gathered the letters and wrapped them with the elastic. I placed them in the box and shoved it off to the side.

I looked over at my laptop and, without another thought, grabbed my computer. I opened Facebook, typed in his name, and without hesitation clicked on the only name that came up. Shock rolled through me when I saw his picture. He was alive. The profile was brand new, but there was no doubt it was him. I hit the message button and began typing, and once I finished, I didn't hesitate. I simply hit send. I then got up off the floor, picked up Sparkles, and headed down the hall to my bedroom.

Morning had come faster than I'd expected, and I'd been dragging myself around ever since. I'd checked my messages a few times already this morning, each time disappointment flooding me at the fact that Noah hadn't even seen the message.

Willow Valley was bustling with shoppers this morning. The shop owners were decorating their windows for their holiday displays, and the town was busy decorating all the light posts. I climbed out of the car and let out a yawn. I needed a coffee before I went to the community center. I crossed the street and pushed the door of The Crispy Biscuit open and walked in, shocked to find the place empty.

"Oh, hey, Mindi," I heard Brooke say, and saw a hand waving at me from behind the counter.

"Hey, Brooke, what's going on? Where is everyone?" I questioned. "I don't recall ever seeing this place empty.

"Oh, it's been a morning, let me tell you. One of the large walk-in refrigerators went in the back, so we had to call in a repairman. However, that also meant that all our baking supplies that were in there spoiled overnight. Tristan has gone into Cedar Landing with Melinda to pick up some things from our supplier."

"Oh, Brooke, I'm so sorry to hear."

"It's okay. Part of owning a business, I guess. Anyway, I have Jack in the back fixing the fridge. I was just going to close the place for the day but figured I could at least do coffee and whatever baked goods I had left over from yesterday. Thankfully, I had all the baking crate orders completed and wrapped up last night, but I've had to put a delay on the ones that came in today. I'm so glad my customers can understand."

"Well, I am thankful for that too, and I'm thankful

you are open for coffee because I need one." I giggled. "And with my coffee, I think I'll take one of those croissants. Oh wait, maybe one of those double fudge cookies."

"How about both? I'll give them to you at fifty percent off."

"You don't need to twist my arm." I giggled.

Brooke laughed as she grabbed a plate. "You know, I think I might sit down and join you."

"I'd love that," I said, removing my coat and hat, moving over to one of the large booths in the store's front window. "Getting ready to do your holiday display?" I questioned.

"Sure am. Tristan hired a local artist as a surprise. They are coming this week to get things started," Brooke said as she slid in across from me after placing a tray down on the table. We each grabbed a croissant and a cookie and a cup of coffee.

"So what's new?" she questioned.

"Not much. I have been busy planning the meal out for the community center for Christmas, so I should have my order to you by the end of this week. I have also been working on the list of things I was thinking we could get for Sarah. I want to make sure we are collecting during the winter festival."

Brooke nodded in agreement. "I couldn't agree more, and you know Tristan and I will have a table there with hot chocolate and goodies. We are always happy to accept donations that night. We could even place a box for gift items as well, in case people want to drop things off. I know Trinity is also happy to help. She was going through some books at the shop, figuring out what she could donate, and she mentioned collecting donations at her table as well."

"Amazing, you two are too good to me," I said, smiling.

"You do a lot for this community, Mindi. Besides, we're always thrilled to lend a hand, no questions asked. Sometimes, we wish we could do more."

"I know you never say no when asked anything, and I thank you for that," I said, taking a sip of my coffee. "I just wish we could find Sarah a family for Christmas. That way she won't have to move to the center after the holidays."

Brooke brought her hand to her chest. "Me too. It's so devastating. I can't imagine what that will do to her. She's been with you for over a year."

"Me either. Willow Valley is the only home she's ever known. Breaks my heart."

"Well, you know, I always say Christmas is a magical time here in Willow Valley. Maybe the magic of the season will grant her a new family. Never say never."

"I hope you are right," I said, giving half a smile. "I wish I could take her in, but they have made it clear they are looking for a home with two parents," I said, letting out a sigh. "I don't suppose you and Tristan are..."

"We've talked about trying again, but we think we are just going to hold off," she said, her expression growing serious.

Brooke and Tristan had been trying to get pregnant, but hadn't been lucky, and they'd begun looking at adopting, but the last two opportunities they'd been given had fallen through at the last minute. She'd mentioned to me more times than not that they were both feeling like maybe a child wasn't in the cards for them.

We both grew quiet, and I looked out the front window to see some crews from the Willow Valley Town Hall putting up the Christmas lights for the festival.

"Soon the town will become a twinkling wonderland," I said, nodding to the men across the street.

"I can't wait, to be honest. I always love looking out at those lights and the displays. Seeing the park filled with kids and people taking part in winter activities has always been one of my favorite parts of the season."

"Mine too." I sighed.

"Mindi, you look tired today. Is everything alright?"

I looked at Brooke, not sure I wanted to tell her what I'd found in the mailbox. We were four years apart, and while we'd been friends when Noah and I had been dating, I'd never really shared many personal things with her from that time in my life. But as we got older, we shared more personal things and we'd grown closer than we'd ever been. She watched me, and when I met her eyes, I could feel my walls breaking down.

"Yeah, things are fine. I think the whole situation with Sarah is getting to me. Plus, I just received something in the mail the other day that has got me a bit rattled."

"Oh, not bad news, I hope."

"No, it's not," I said, clearing my throat and taking a mouthful of coffee. "Do you remember Noah?"

Brooke lifted her eyes to mine and gave me a funny look. "Sure do. You guys were so close, I remember wondering if we'd hear wedding bells once he returned." She smiled. "Did you ever find out what really happened to him?"

I swallowed hard. No one really knew what had happened to him. Everyone just followed my lead and assumed he'd died, especially after his parents had left. It was the only real reason we had for him not returning and his parents leaving.

"No, but he isn't dead," I said, releasing the only information I had found.

"What? What do you mean?"

"When you are close to someone, you somehow have an unspoken connection. While I chose the only option that made sense to me, and one that made it easier to cope with, I never really believed he was gone. It was like my soul could still feel him."

"Sounds like you've been taking a stroll down memory lane lately," Brooke said with a gentle smile.

"You could say that. I mean, it is that time of year. It started when I got home the other day. I found one of those bags in the mailbox. You know, the ones that they put mail in when either the contents of the envelope go missing or get damaged or lost."

Brooke nodded, waiting for me to continue.

"Well, inside that bag was a Christmas card from 2015. It was from Noah."

"What! That is crazy. After all these years, it finally got to you."

"Yes, and do you know what he'd written inside?"

Brooke shook her head, waiting for me to continue.

"He proposed to me."

"What????"

"I guess he must have sent it after the last letter I received from him."

"Why do you think that?"

"I don't know. I just know the letter I received was the last letter I'd gotten from him, despite writing him for an entire year, which to be honest, I don't know why I continued because he never got any of them, they were all returned to me."

"I remember that Christmas. You were so excited that he was coming home, and then you were so heartbroken when he couldn't make it, and then in January when he didn't appear, you were even worse. Then, his parents left. Do you remember the following year I tried to set you up with Billy Parsons? You remember that?"

"Sure do. We hit it off for a bit, but I was still having a hard time getting over Noah. Or maybe I wasn't ready to." I smiled and then grew serious again.

It was then that tears formed in my eyes. My eyes burned as I looked at Brooke and swallowed. I picked up my mug and took a sip, and then ripped off a piece of the buttery croissant and shoved it into my mouth.

"Did you hear from him after that, at any point over the years?"

I shook my head. "No, even after his parents returned, they wouldn't speak to me, and here I was questioning why. I guess I know the answer to that now." I shrugged.

"Well, did you ask Ethan? Perhaps he knew him or knows someone who does."

"I was going to but decided against it. Brooke, I am not sure I want the whole town talking about it again. I lived through that once, through the looks every time I walked into a building or went to an event, the whispers behind my back. I've given it a lot of thought today. What if this was how it was supposed to be?"

"I don't understand?"

"What if we were just supposed to part ways? Maybe we weren't supposed to be married, or to date any longer than we did. I'm not sure I want to revisit an old path, open up old wounds. For what? To find out that they will end the same way anyway?"

Brooke sighed. "If I had thought that way, then Tristan and I would never have gotten together."

"The pair of you were different. There probably always was something between you that you couldn't see. There'd be nothing between us now, not after I hurt him the way I did."

"Perhaps, but you'll never know unless you contact him."

My fingers ran around the rim of my mug as I sat there thinking about what she'd just said.

"I already know, Brooke."

"How?"

"I looked him up on Facebook. I found him there. I sent a message, and he hasn't even read it."

"When did you send it?"

Again, I ran my fingers around the rim of my mug. "Last night."

"Give him a chance. He might just be as shocked as you are. I mean, given the circumstances."

"It was a stupid idea to reach out," I said, trying to make a heavy situation lighter. "It's not a wonder he didn't return home. I probably ripped his heart out."

"Mindi, you didn't hurt him intentionally. You didn't know he sent that card. It's not like you rejected his proposal."

"That is true. I just think it was dumb to message him. I mean, what am I supposed to say? Sorry for hurting you by never responding to your proposal?"

"While that is not how you should start things, it actually might be a good idea to at least let him know why you are contacting him, by telling him you received the card ten years too late."

"I don't think so."

"Can I ask you what it is you're afraid of?"

I studied her and then finally let out the breath I was holding. "Finding out that his life didn't turn out like mine."

Brooke frowned at me. "What is that supposed to mean? Your life turned out fine. You own a successful tree farm, you're part of a wonderful community that cherishes you. You have many friends who love you."

"That is true, but there is one thing I don't have, and that is someone to go home to every night."

Brooke smiled. "I didn't have that either for years, might I remind you? I think you should take a chance and try to find him. There is only one way to know how things turned out for him, and contacting him would be it. The worst thing that could happen is finding out he's in a committed relationship. At least you will know, and it will put an end to your suffering."

As if on cue, the doors opened, and the little bell

above the door jingled. Brooke looked over toward the door and then back at me.

"I have to go. Enjoy your coffee and croissant and, for goodness' sakes, take a chance. It is a magical season, after all. Who knows, perhaps come the new year we will not only have a home for Sarah, but we might just have a wedding to plan."

"Ha, that's hilarious, and I'm not talking about the Sarah part." I giggled.

"Never say never." She winked.

"Well, whatever you do, please don't hold your breath." I giggled. "And I will enjoy because I need your sweets to get through the rest of this year." I winked.

She gave me a quick hug and then took off over behind the counter and quickly looked after her customers while I sat there, drowning my sorrows in my cup of coffee and the rest of my buttery pastry.

Noah

I'd been in my new place a week and had gotten things mostly unpacked and situated, which meant I'd barely left the house. I had to change that, so I called up Clay to see if he was available for a coffee, since he and Iris were the only people I'd gotten acquainted with since moving back. He spoke to Iris and, a few moments later, agreed to meet me late this morning at The Crispy Biscuit.

I took off out the door and began walking toward the downtown strip. It had been years since I'd walked these streets, but I remembered most of them instantly.

It was good to see that Bluebird Books was still in business, and I wondered if Vi still owned it or if she'd finally retired. I made a mental note to stop in and visit, perhaps pick up a new read. I also wanted to check out the community center. I wanted to find out more about the counselor position and drop off the donation I had for the food drive, and also to see if they were still looking for help with the holiday elves. Since I was early, I headed there first.

I pulled the large brown door open and entered. Laughter rang out down the hall, and a few kids took off running past me. I couldn't help but smile.

"Can I help you?" I heard a man's voice say from behind me.

I turned and smiled, then held out my hand.

"Hey, I'm Noah Lucas."

"Nice to meet you, Noah. I'm Ethan Alexander, one of the retired military volunteers here. What brings you in today?" he asked, shaking my hand.

"Well, I'm relatively new to the area, or, should I say, a returning resident. I grew up in Willow Valley, and I, too, am a retired military officer. I was in the grocery store the other night and saw that you were looking for help for both the holiday elves, and after speaking with the cashier, I learned you are also looking for a counselor. Plus, I have this for the food drive," I said, holding up a small bag of canned goods and some pasta.

"Well, first, welcome home."

"Thank you," I answered.

"Now, about the holiday elves program. We certainly could use help. Unfortunately, there are more kids and families enrolled in the program than ever before, so the more hands we have, the more we will achieve. My daughter Melinda, who works over at the Crispy Biscuit, is one of the head elves, and I know she will be thrilled to know that she will have one extra hand. As for the counselor position, do you know someone who would fit the job?"

"Yes, sure do. Before I left the military, I had been struggling. I took some time off, got treatment, and then put my focus on getting educated. I wanted to help others who were struggling like me. So, I did the courses and got my license to counsel with the military."

"That's wonderful. Are you currently working?"

I shook my head. "Unfortunately, in moving back, I left my current job hoping to find one here. So if the position is still available, I'd sure love a chance of applying."

Ethan nodded and stepped out of the way of the five kids who flew past me when I walked into the center.

"Guys, slow down there," he called after them.

"Sorry, Ethan!" one of them shouted back.

"I'd love to know where they get that energy from." Ethan chuckled, turning his attention back to me.

"Same. What I could do with that again!" I laughed.

"Seriously!" Ethan chuckled. "Now, for the job. You'd not only be working with people in the military, but you'd mostly be with kids. We find that some of them are really struggling, especially with the holidays, so that is why we put the call out for a counselor."

"That isn't a problem. I've worked with kids at my last post."

"That is good to know. Mindi, who looks after the program here, isn't in right now. She had to step out and do a few errands, but she should be back later this afternoon. You could always stop by and speak with her."

I felt my heart skip a beat at the sound of her name. Could it be true? Was it my Mindi who was running the center? She'd always been involved with the community when we were younger, and I'd remembered her working with this type of program years ago before.

"What do you say?" I heard Ethan ask.

"About?" I questioned, feeling silly that I'd allowed my mind to wander.

"Stopping back in this afternoon. It's been so hard to find a good fit for the team. I'm certain Mindi would sit down and speak with you."

I could feel my pulse in my throat as I nodded. "I can certainly stop back in," I said.

"Sounds good. I'll let her know you are planning on coming back in today or tomorrow at the latest, in case you get sidetracked, but I certainly hope we will see you again."

"Sure will," I said, holding my hand out for Ethan to shake once again.

The cold air hit me as I stepped out the door of the community center. My mind wandered right back to where it was when I'd gotten sidetracked. Could it actually be my Mindi? I wondered. Had she really never left Willow Valley? Was this fate's way of dropping her back into my life after all these years? How was I going to approach this? Should I just run now and not come back?

I shook my head. I needed to clear my thoughts. So what if it was Mindi who ran the program at the center? We were adults, not a pair of teens. Everything was in the past. She'd denied me, and that was okay. I'd gotten over it and moved on. I knew things had been hard on her when I was gone, so it hadn't surprised me. What had surprised me was that she hadn't reached out at least to tell me, but again, I had moved past that, hadn't I?

I let out a sigh, glanced at my watch, and noticed I still had an hour before I was to meet up with Clay. I glanced across the street at a small boutique shop, Treasures and Gifts. It must be a new store because I didn't remember it being there when I was younger, so I went to check it out. I needed a gift for my niece, anyway.

I took off across the street and pulled the door open, stepping inside the small store. A woman behind the counter smiled in my direction but was with a customer, so I just smiled back and went about looking at things for myself.

I took my time looking over the shelves, seeking some sort of idea for a ten-year-old girl who I'd not seen in five years. My brother had sent me a few things she'd like, but I wanted to get her something from me, like I used to, and not something just picked off a list I was given.

I slowly wandered into the back of the store and rounded the corner...and stopped in my tracks. I couldn't believe my eyes. Was it really her?

I blinked and wiped at my eyes. I wanted to pinch myself to see if I was actually dreaming. There in front of me was Mindi. She stood there, picking up one candle after another, smelling them with a soft smile on her face. God, she looked the same. Her picture on social media hadn't really done her justice. She was as beautiful as ever.

I stood there watching her, my pulse racing. God, I wanted to approach her, to talk to her, but my feet were glued to the floor. There was no way I could just approach her out of the blue like that.

She put the candle she'd been smelling down and was about to turn around and face me, so I stepped into another aisle, hopefully hiding out of sight. I strolled away from her when I heard a man say her name. The moment I heard her laugh, I knew without a doubt it was her. Her laugh, like music to my ears, hadn't changed.

I made my way to the end of the aisle and poked my head around the corner. His hand rested on her lower back as they spoke low to one another, and then they both laughed.

At that moment, my heart sank. I wasn't sure what it was I was expecting by seeing her again, but somewhere deep inside me, disappointment hit. I felt ridiculous feeling the way I did; I guess somewhere inside of me I'd hoped that everything had been a misunderstanding and that when and if we crossed paths again, it would have been like the last ten years hadn't happened.

"Sir, is there something I can help you find?" I heard a woman ask from behind me.

It was then I realized I was crouched down on the ground.

"Ah, yes, I was just trying to find something for my niece." I smiled.

"Well, how old is she?"

"Ten."

"Well, come on over here and let's see what we have."

The woman led me over near the window, and while she pulled things from the shelf, I watched Mindi walk by.

Mindi

One Week Later

A gust of blustery winter air blew as I pulled the doors open and stepped inside. Christmas music played lightly over the gentle chatter of the residents of Willow Valley as they had their coffees.

"Morning, Mindi!" Brooke sang from behind the counter as she slid two trays of the holiday cookies she'd made into the display case.

"Morning! Busy this morning! Can I get a coffee, and two of those delicious-looking Santa cookies for here and two to go, please?"

"Of course! I heard that the food drive went well! Ethan said it was one of the best turnouts."

"It did, and I think he is right. I think it really was the

best turnout we've ever had, to be honest. So many people came out to show their support."

"That is fantastic. You should be proud. All your hard work paid off."

I smiled, not liking when others said it was all to do with me, because it took a community to accomplish what we had. I was only a cog on the giant wheel, and it was all because of them it had been a success.

"I am proud. Proud to be part of a community like this," I said, smiling. "I'd never be able to pull it off without all of you. Now, that being said, I'm going to sit down with my coffee and cookies and work on the holiday menu for the kids. That way, you can prepare the items I'll be needing from you," I said, smiling as I picked up my coffee and cookies.

"Stay as long as you want. Just signal when you want a refill." Brooke smiled as Tristan stepped out carrying two more trays of cookies.

"Morning, Mindi! I'm gonna come by and pick up the trees tonight if that is okay." He smiled.

"Sure thing! I might not be home if you come too early. Sarah and I have some errands to run tonight. If I'm not home yet, just let Connor know you are taking them. He'll be out cutting a few more down tonight. We sold out yesterday, but yours are marked and have been placed aside."

"Sounds good."

I smiled and took off toward one of the few empty tables in the diner. I pulled the papers from my bag and placed them in piles, thinking back to the event yesterday. While it had gone wonderfully, I felt like I was losing my mind. I still hadn't heard a word from Noah—my message had gone completely unread—but I could have sworn I saw him a few times yesterday in the crowd. Of course, each time I saw him, someone interrupted me and pulled my attention away. When I turned back around, he was gone.

I'd gone home last night, put Sarah to bed, and then pulled out all of his letters again, re-reading them, and then I went to the message I'd sent to see it was still unread, then I deleted it and focused on the paperwork in front of me, working until the wee hours of the morning, and now I needed to get through this menu and figure out what it was I was missing.

"More coffee?"

I only nodded, afraid that if I looked up from what I was working on, I'd lose my concentration.

"Ha, I told Tristan you'd want cinnamon rolls." She smiled as she looked over the list I'd been working on.

"Of course I'd want those." I giggled as Brooke filled my mug. "I'd have to be crazy not to have those on the menu. Not only were they the holiday winner, but they are a holiday favorite now. I think if you were to take them off the menu, the town would revolt."

"I know. I might have started a small cinnamon roll cult."

"Oh, I meant to ask, how is Sarah?"

"Good, really good. We are getting ready to decorate her room tonight; she's really excited. I should have you put two cinnamon buns into a box for dessert tonight, along with those cookies."

"Good to hear, and no problem. I'll add them right away." Brooke patted my shoulder and then turned to continue refilling other's mugs when I heard her welcome someone. It was then I'd remembered one other thing I'd been missing and jotted it down, not paying attention to who she was speaking to. I let out a sigh and placed my pencil down on the table, picking up my coffee. I was about to take a sip when a familiar scent of cologne enveloped me.

Memories flooded my mind as I inhaled deeply. There was only one person I knew who wore that cologne, and there was no way he was here. It wasn't possible... My mind was playing tricks on me again. It was only because I'd just spent the last few days looking over Noah's letters that I would have even remembered that scent. Some letters, even though it was faint, still smelled exactly like him. It was the same as yesterday, his letters; that was the only reason I'd thought I'd seen him.

I shook my head and went to pick up my pencil and

get back to working on the menu when I felt a warm hand on my shoulder.

I froze as my eyes fell to the hand that rested on my shoulder, and I slowly raised my head to see a pair of bluish-gray eyes staring back at me. With my heart in my throat, I focused on the person standing in front of me. It couldn't be.

Surprise and shock filled my body as our eyes met. He looked different. He'd filled out, his body more muscular and inviting. His eyes, though, held a sorrow I'd never seen in them before. He definitely wasn't the same boy who had left here all those years ago, eyes bright and excited. The military had changed him.

As we stood there looking into one another's eyes, every feeling and emotion I'd suppressed over the years fought to come to the surface. I wanted to know everything that had happened in his life from the last time we talked until now; I wanted to share everything with him that had happened in mine, but I had to keep it under control.

It had been ten years since we'd stood in front of one another, but one look in his eyes and I could feel the same pull he'd had on me back then.

Noah

She studied me for what felt like forever. It was okay; I didn't expect her to jump into my arms after all these years. She'd aged well, and if it was possible, she was even more beautiful than she'd been when we were younger.

I looked into her eyes, the same soft, loving eyes I'd remembered looking into the day I'd left on my first deployment. It felt like we'd been transported back in time. The only thing that had changed out of all this was that we'd gotten older. Otherwise, standing here, looking at her, everything felt the same. I could feel my feelings rise to the surface, but knew I'd never be able to stand to have my heart broken again. I didn't know if the fact we never got closure had to do with my being single or not, but it was something I'd always wondered.

"Ugh, how rude of me," she murmured before smiling. "Would you like to join me for a coffee?" she asked, her voice shaking.

Was she nervous? Was that what the shake in her voice was?

"I'd love to," I said, still staring into those eyes. "I've grown very fond of this place again."

"One moment."

I watched as she made her way over to the counter, then leaned across it and whispered something to the dark-haired woman I knew as Melinda. She waited while Melinda poured a cup of coffee and then brought it over to the table. She placed it down on the opposite side and quickly began clearing the papers from the table.

"Thank you," I said, clearing my throat as I sat down across from her.

She didn't look at me. Instead, she fiddled with the papers that had been piled on the table and shoved them messily into a file folder and then slid the cup over to me, while reaching for the sugar and creamer that sat on the table, and placed them in the center before she sat down.

"So, how have you been, Mindi?" I questioned, wanting her to raise her beautiful eyes to me again.

"Okay," she answered softly, "and you?"

"Doing well now," I answered. "I moved back to Willow Valley a month ago."

I couldn't make out what she was thinking, but I

could tell from her expression that she was curious about something.

"What is it?" I questioned.

"You've been back a month. How have we not seen one another until now?"

I dumped a creamer into my coffee and met her eyes again. "I'm not sure. I've been busy getting settled and looking for work. To be honest, I wasn't even sure you'd still be in the area."

"What sort of work are you looking for? Perhaps I could help?" she asked.

Just like that, there was the Mindi I knew, the girl who would always help someone in need. Suddenly, it didn't feel like any time had passed at all.

"Funny you should ask that. I stopped over at the community center, but I apparently missed someone named Mindi. I've been looking for a counselor position."

She lifted her eyes to mine.

"Are you the Mindi I'm supposed to speak with?"

"I am, and you're the man who was supposed to stop by but didn't? Ethan told me about you, but he never mentioned a name."

I nodded. "I am."

She didn't take her eyes off me. She swallowed, and her hand shook as she took a sip of her coffee. "We need a counselor badly."

"Perhaps we could sit down and talk soon," I said, watching as she placed her mug back down on the table.

"I think we could, although there isn't any doubt in my mind that you'd do a fantastic job."

"Tell me a little about the community center. What do you do there?"

"Well, aside from all community events, I have focused on helping families who are in the military, just like I did when you left. I have recently put in place a children's program to help kids whose parent or parents have been deployed. I wanted them to have a place to make friends so they wouldn't feel so alone and to take their minds off their situation. It helps them to be around those who are dealing with the same things. We do craft days and provide meals for them on holidays and help with all community events. Honestly, I've just worked and built upon the program that I began when you left."

"I always loved that about you. After all these years, you still want to help others, more times than not putting other's needs above yours."

I could barely take my eyes off her. After all this time, she was in front of me, and I feared if I looked away she'd be gone. I listened to her tell me all about the other programs, and just like that, it felt like I'd never left her.

"You know, I really love giving back, but the past couple of years, I think I have taken on more than I can handle."

"Why do you say that?"

She studied me, almost as if she were wondering if she should answer me. Then she let out the breath she was holding and held onto her coffee cup.

"Well, one family here suffered a tragedy last year. Sarah, she's a sweet girl, one I've gotten to know over the years at the center. Her parents, both military, were deployed at the end of the summer. They were both killed in an ambush in September. Sarah had no relatives, and since I am one of the approved caretakers, she moved in with me. It was a challenge to help her deal with the loss, and now this year, sadly, she will be put up for adoption in the new year. Since things don't move fast with the military, they still don't have anyone, but she will move into an approved foster facility until she is adopted. Everyone thought it was best for her to be in a familiar set of surroundings while she dealt with the loss, but it's literally killing me. I'd like to do more for her since Willow Valley is the only home she's ever known."

"Her last name happen to be Lancaster?" I questioned.

"Yes, how did you know?"

"I knew Heidi and John very well."

"This is probably the hardest situation I've been in," she said, avoiding my eyes for a moment.

"Have you tried finding someone here in Willow Valley that may want to adopt her?"

Mindi nodded. "I have, but the things they are looking for practically weed out every family in the area. I'd take her myself, but they want a two-parent household. Ethan, whom you met, just tells me to take a breath and take things one day at a time, that things will work out. I just fear that it won't, and she'll have to move away."

"You know Ethan is right."

"I do."

"Good, because years ago someone told me the same thing."

She studied me, and then a small and knowing smile came to her lips.

"You're right. I just want to make sure she is okay. She's lost so much."

"She has, but trust me when I say these kids are resilient."

"I know that too. Sometimes, I hate that I always want to make sure others are alright."

"Yes, I remember. Your letters never talked about how much you missed me until the very end of the letter. After a while, I wondered if you were just saying you missed me so I didn't feel you weren't."

"Please tell me you aren't serious?"

"I am."

"If I went on and on about how much I missed you, monopolizing the entire letter with my feelings, when I knew you were struggling with being away from home, what sort of girlfriend would I have been?"

"A normal one, and one who wasn't afraid to let someone else know how she felt." I winked.

"I wasn't afraid of how I felt. I just didn't want to make things harder for you while you were gone. I knew it was a struggle for you to be away from home."

"It was, but, Mindi, what sort of man would I be if I couldn't handle how you felt as well. We were in what I thought was a serious relationship, one in which we could talk about anything, even in the tough times. I knew you were struggling, even if you didn't want to say it. I often worried about how you were handling things."

"You're acting as if I never told you how I was feeling. It's not like I never did; I just didn't want to make it an issue," she said, bringing her hands to her chest.

"I know, I just had to get smart and read between the lines." I winked.

We both grew quiet and picked up our coffee and took a drink. There was only one question on the tip of my tongue at the moment, and I knew I needed an answer to it, or else I might as well just get up from this table right now and walk out. There was no point in my sitting here talking with her any further about our past without an answer. I was certain that we deserved another chance; why else would she still be here all these years later? If this moment taught me anything, it's that some feelings never fade and that just because the timing wasn't right in the past, it didn't mean it's never the right time. The moment my cup was back on the table, I looked over at her and cleared my throat.

"Are you seeing anyone?" I questioned. I needed to know. If she was, that was fine, at least I'd know not to pursue things with her any further. I'd take a few days, and then I'd go into the center and apply for the counselor position.

She studied me and then shook her head.

"What about you? Married?"

I didn't answer, but I'd gotten the answer I needed. I figured she'd get her answer with the next couple of questions I asked, especially if she were still as perceptive as she used to be.

"Won't they be having the tree lighting soon?" I questioned, looking over across the street where I could see some men still working on stringing lights in the enormous park. "I remember it was always around this time of year."

"Yes, it's on Friday, always on the first day of December."

"Well then, how about we meet that night? Say at the pavilion in the center of the park. I'll stop and get us some hot chocolate. We can go ice skating; we'll catch up. You can tell me about the type of counselor you are looking for, and we will take it from there."

Her eyes met mine. Shock lined them as she stared back at me. She was still as perceptive as she once had been. She knew exactly what I was asking.

"What do you say? Will you meet me?"

She stared back at me. I could feel my heart pounding in my chest as I waited for her answer.

"How does six thirty sound?" I urged, afraid that a no was on the edge of her lips.

I did not know why I wasn't letting this go. Perhaps it was because after all these years, she was sitting in front of me. Maybe it was the fact that she was single, and I could get my second chance with her. After all, the first chance we'd had was cut somewhat short. Maybe everything had been a misunderstanding. I didn't know.

"I will see you then," she said, her eyes finally falling to the table and away from me.

I wasn't giving her a chance to change her mind. I drank down the rest of my coffee, got up, and grabbed my jacket.

"I have some errands to run, but I will see you then." I smiled and then turned and made my way out of The Crispy Biscuit, leaving her sitting there.

With my heart in my throat, I drove home.

I'd had to get away from her and clear my thoughts.

Mindi hadn't changed a bit. She was still the same woman I'd fallen in love with all those years ago. She was still shy in most ways, and still had a heart of gold that I'd give anything to own. The best part was that she'd never lost sight of herself, nor what she believed in. That was clear. She had always been determined to help others, and by the looks of things, she was still doing it.

Her heart was the part of her I'd loved the most, and what had originally brought me to her.

I parked the car in the driveway and made my way into the house. I took off my jacket and headed to the kitchen, where I grabbed a soda from the fridge. Why had I avoided the one question I really wanted an answer to? I should have just asked her about the Christmas card I'd sent. Why hadn't I asked her why she'd never responded? Was I afraid of her answer? Damn right I was.

I hadn't been sure I was ready to talk to her, yet she'd sat there in front of me, within arm's reach, my body aching to touch her. Until I'd set eyes on her, I hadn't realized how badly I still wanted a chance with her. Somehow, even though that had been a burning question in the back of my mind, I'd been willing to put that question on pause. I didn't want to scare her away by being angry, or forcing her to answer a question that perhaps she wasn't ready to.

Perhaps this chance was presented to us to realize we could start over, and I knew that if I wanted this to be our second chance together, I had to take things slowly and perhaps overlook the past. It was the only way I could see us moving on. Harboring all the feelings I'd held onto about that card, the lack of response, had almost killed me, and I knew I had to let that all go if ever we were to have even a slight chance at a second time together.

Mindi

I'd taken Sarah over to Bluebird Books for Iris's reading program earlier this morning and then realized I had forgotten the box of decorations I'd pulled up from the basement last night for the community center sitting on the kitchen table, so I'd had to come back home.

I waved to the boys who were manning my tree lot this year as I pulled out of the driveway for the second time this morning. If it hadn't been for Connor and Gabe talking with their farmhands, I'd never have found their kids. The four boys I'd hired to look after everything had been doing a wonderful job. People were getting their trees and it had freed me up to be present while the kids at the community center got to decorate the gazebo in the center of the park.

Once back at the community center, I carried a pile of

boxes up from the basement and into the gymnasium, where Peggy and Ethan were working away, sorting things out. "I think these are the last boxes," I said, placing them down on one table.

"Wonderful," Peggy said, grabbing one off the top. "Hopefully, the spare Christmas lights are inside here."

"If they aren't in one of those, then I think we may have run out. I can always text Brooke and have her grab some before she and Tristan come over."

"No need, I found them," Ethan said, holding up the spare bulbs he'd found inside the tote he'd been emptying.

"Perfect, I'll be back in a moment. I'm just going to grab the tape from my office along with the plan we have designed for the gazebo," I said, flying out of the gymnasium door and down the hall.

Ethan and Peggy had come over early, since the flower shop was closed today, and had helped me get some things out and organized before the kids arrived. Trinity and Thomas would be here any minute, and Brooke and Tristan had decided they'd join us as well, allowing Melinda to run The Crispy Biscuit for the day. I glanced at my watch, seeing that most of the kids would be here to help shortly, and we wanted to be ready for them.

I dug through my top desk drawer, grabbed the tape, and then took off back toward the gym. I let out a scream as I rounded the corner and ran right into someone.

"Oh gosh, Mindi, are you alright?" I heard a familiar voice say, and felt hands grab my upper arms.

It took me a minute to get myself together, and then I looked up into Noah's blue eyes.

"Sorry about that. I wasn't expecting you to come bolting out of that door."

"I wasn't expecting anyone to be in the hallway." I giggled, brushing my hair back out of my face.

"Ethan told me you guys were decorating the gazebo in the park today and told me I should stop by. Hope that is okay."

"Of course," I said, smiling. "Come on."

We were just about down the hall to the gymnasium door when the front doors opened and a group of kids came running in.

"Hey, everyone," I called, smiling.

"Hey, Mindi!" one boy called out first, followed by the rest of the kids.

"Head on into the gym." I smiled, watching as they dumped their coats onto the floor as usual.

Just as the last two ran by Noah and me, the front door opened again, and I saw Sarah come inside, Iris glued to her side, tears streaming down her face. I turned to Noah.

"Can you give me a few minutes? That is Sarah, who's staying with me, the one who lost her parents," I whispered.

"Of course, I'll head on into the gym and see what I can help with," he said with a wink.

I made my way down the hall toward Sarah, and Iris and smiled softly. "How are you doing?" I questioned, looking up at Iris.

Iris shook her head while I kneeled down so I was eye-level with Sarah. Almost immediately, she wrapped her arms around my neck, hugging me tight.

"Hey, sweetheart," I whispered, hugging her back.

I was at a loss for how to respond to her; I did not know how to help at this point. Mostly, she had dealt with everything well; it was just in the last couple of days that she'd cried more often than not.

"We thought we'd come and see if perhaps there was something Sarah could help with today," Iris said.

"I think we could find something," I said, walking her down to the gymnasium door and grabbing Peggy right away.

Once Sarah was working away with Peggy, I turned to see Iris standing beside me.

"What happened?" I questioned.

"Sarah just broke down in tears," Iris whispered. "She just wanted to come here."

I looked over at Sarah, her face expressionless, which made me wonder if she had finally realized the holidays were here and that after the holidays she'd be moving, which possibly could have compounded the effects of losing her parents. It was then that Sarah left Peggy and came running over to me, wrapping her arms around my waist.

"Did you want to help me with putting together and decorating two trees for the gazebo?" I questioned.

Sarah said nothing; she just stood there hugging me tighter. I looked at Iris with concern.

"What about helping me get the lights ready to put up? We are going with the suggestion you gave me the other night. Red and green this year, which means we need to make sure the colors alternate properly," I said, thinking that may make her smile, only once again, there wasn't anything.

"What about the garland?" I asked. "Gracie is coming over shortly to help. Did you want to help us with that? We really could use the help; the boys around the center don't want to do the silly girl things." I winked, hoping to get at least a glimmer of a smile from her.

Defeat filled me as she once again just stared at me.

"What about helping me decorate some cookies?" I heard Noah ask behind me.

I turned and met his gaze, catching a wink from him.

"Brooke and Tristan brought over all the cookies, icing and decorations for us to use. We can make them as silly or as serious as you'd like, with fun sayings, or even some funny faces, even sad faces, because sometimes people are sad at Christmas. Then tomorrow night, once the music starts, Brooke and Tristan will hand out hot chocolate and cider, and we can be in charge of handing out the cookies."

I looked down at Sarah and then back to Noah. I couldn't help but wonder what he was up to when I heard Sarah speak for the first time.

"Can we make sad snowmen and happy snowmen?" she asked quietly.

"Absolutely we can," he answered.

Sarah looked up at Iris and me and slowly let go of my waist and went over to Noah, who kneeled down so he could meet her eye to eye. They shared some words quietly between them, and then he stood up and took her hand in his and together they headed into the gymnasium, over to the cookie decorating table.

I turned to Iris, not really knowing what to say about what we'd just witnessed, but whatever it was, I hoped it was going to be good for Sarah.

"Oh, I was thinking if Sarah wanted to come over and spend the night next weekend, just let us know. Gracie and she have been talking about a sleepover."

"Thanks, Iris," I said, walking her over to the door. "I'll talk with her tonight and let you know."

"Wonderful. I'll see you soon with the boys and Gracie."

"Sounds good."

When I walked into the gymnasium, everyone was

already hard at work getting decorations together and ready to put up. Christmas music was playing, some kids were singing, while others focused on the task at hand. It was then I glanced over to see Noah and Sarah hard at work decorating the cookies Brooke had brought over. To my surprise, Sarah was talking Noah's ear off, and when he looked up and over at me, he winked. Whatever he'd done, whatever he'd said, he was getting her to talk, which was what she needed the most, and for that alone, I was grateful to him.

Noah

I parked the truck in the only spot I could find and hopped out. It appeared we had taken the last nice evening last night while decorating the gazebo because sometime overnight it had grown super cold and snow now blanketed Willow Valley, giving the park a beautiful glow.

I could see people on the man-made rink the town had put up since the small lake hadn't frozen over yet. I grabbed my gloves and skates before leaving the truck. It had been so long since I'd skated, I hoped I hadn't forgotten how.

Skating used to be our thing every winter when we were younger. It had actually been our very first date in this very park at this very event. I smiled as the memory filled my mind.

I glanced at my watch, it was almost six thirty, and I

couldn't help but wonder if Mindi was already here. It wouldn't look good if I was late, so I quickly made my way over to where Brooke and Tristan were serving the first batch of hot chocolate and apple cider before the tree lighting.

"Hey, Noah, what can I get for you?" Brooke asked as I approached the table.

"Two hot chocolates, please, and two cookies," I answered.

She got right to pouring the two cups while Tristan bagged the cookies Sarah and I had decorated.

"So, how does it feel being back in your old hometown?" Tristan asked, handing me the cookies.

"Honestly, it feels very much like home. Not a lot has changed, but it has at the same time," I added.

"It was nice to have you helping at the community center the other day as well," Brooke said. "I'm sure Mindi appreciated that."

"It was nice to be included," I told her. "Have you seen her?"

"Not yet," Brooke said, passing me the two cups of hot chocolate.

A feeling of disappointment fell over me, wondering if perhaps she would not show.

"There she is." Tristan smiled. "She's walking over with Trinity and Thomas right now," he said, holding his arm up in the air and waving in their direction.

"They all know where we set up, silly." Brooke giggled, elbowing Tristan in the side.

Tristan turned to me, his face screwed up like he was in pain as he rubbed his side. Brooke giggled, and we both laughed. Then he grabbed her and pulled her to his side and kissed her forehead.

"I bet it's odd seeing Mindi again after all these years," Brooke said, pouring herself a cup of hot chocolate and taking a sip.

"No, not odd," I said, my voice low. "Unexpected, but wonderful at the same time." I turned to see her laughing at something Trinity had said. Just as they approached the table, she turned her eyes on me and softly smiled. "Hey you," she whispered.

"Hey, are you ready?" I questioned.

"For…"

"Skating," I said, tugging on one skate that hung over her shoulder.

She nodded and took the hot chocolate from my hand.

"Where's Sarah?" Brooke asked.

"Oh, she is with Gracie and Iris. They are on their way."

"Wonderful," Brooke said, rubbing her hands together.

"Shall we?" Noah asked, slipping his hand into mine

and gently tugging me toward the ice rink as we left Brooke, Tristan, Trinity, and Thomas together.

We'd both just finished tying our skates when I slipped the hot chocolate from her hand and stood up, taking her hands in mine.

"Ready?" I questioned, stepping onto the ice.

"Gosh, Noah, I don't know," she said, looking at the ice in panic. "I haven't done this in years." She giggled. "What if I fall? I'm not as young as I used to be."

"You'll be fine. It will come flying back in no time," I said, hoping I was right, because I too hadn't skated in years. "Besides, I've got you." I winked, hoping I sounded confident and not afraid of both of us falling to the ground.

"Easy for you to say." She giggled.

"Trust me," I said, pulling her to her feet.

The moment her feet hit the ice, she slipped a little, and I quickly slipped in behind her, helping her to regain her balance.

"Just as I remember, it's slippery and I'm as unbalanced as ever." She giggled, grabbing my arm again to regain her balance as she pushed off with her right foot.

Soon, we were talking away as we made our way around the rink. Mindi was telling me about the tree farm when I felt her hand tense against mine. I turned just in time to see her lose her balance but was able to get in behind her just before she hit the ground.

"Thank goodness you were right here," she whispered, her breath against my neck as I held her close to me.

"Told you to trust me," I whispered as I pulled her back up, the scent of her perfume invading my senses.

She met my eyes as she turned in my arms. It was at that moment, under the stars and surrounded by twinkling light, I leaned forward and pressed my lips to hers for the first time in years.

Our lips only connected for seconds before she pulled hers away from mine and placed her hands on my chest and slowly raised her eyes to mine.

"Noah," she whispered breathlessly.

I could feel the connection between us, the same way it had been before I left all those years ago, the protectiveness I felt once upon a time, and I knew that even though I crossed the first line and kissed her, we needed to take things slow, otherwise those feelings would overwhelm the both of us. I hadn't realized how much I missed her in my life, until now, as she stood here staring back at me.

"What is it?" I asked.

She looked at me like she wanted to say something, but she shook her head and pressed her lips to mine once again before we pushed off from where we were standing and circled the ice again.

We made a couple more rounds, and when we got to where we started, I pulled her over to the edge and helped her off the ice and to sit down. I bent down and undid my skates while she did the same.

"How come you ended our skating?" she questioned, looking at me as she slipped her socked foot into her boot.

"Well, it's almost time for us to meet over at the gazebo for the caroling and to finish handing out the cookies we decorated. Plus, I figured you might like to grab a quick bite to eat before we head over," I said, nodding toward where Zach and Iris were busy barbecuing burgers for everyone, while Sarah and Gracie helped with the buns.

"Actually, I'm starved." She giggled as she waved at Iris.

"Well then, shall we?" I asked.

Mindi nodded, gathered up her skates, and then slipped her hand into mine as we made our way over to them.

Mindi

The entire town gathered at the Gazebo for carols, hot chocolate, and sweet treats. Some kids continued skating while others gathered for the tree lighting. The entire crowd erupted in applause as I plugged the lights in and flipped the switch. Soon everyone was singing carols around the tree.

"Well, that was another successful event," I said, grabbing another cookie from the basket Sarah was holding as the crowd dispersed.

"Sure was, and we are out of hot chocolate again," Brooke sang as Trinity and Thomas came over and stood with us. "Pretty much perfect timing."

"How did donations go?" I questioned them both, nodding toward Sarah for them to remember not to say too much.

"Box was overflowing at my table," Trinity added. "Thomas put the box in the car just before we came over."

"Yeah, I'll bring it over to the center in the morning."

"Perfect. I should be there around noon to get ready for our gingerbread house decorating day." I smiled.

"Tristan ran the one that was here at home as well. It was full as well He will pop by tomorrow afternoon,"

Sarah smiled up at me. "Who were we collecting for this year? I missed it, but I have a few things that I could donate. I've outgrown some of my toys and some clothes, plus when the time comes to leave, I won't be able to take much with me other than a couple of items."

My heart almost ripped in two as I looked down at her. I couldn't tell her she was the recipient, but I also couldn't turn away her donation. She'd always donated something to the drive.

"I didn't have time to get them, but I will, I promise. I'll bring them to the community center tomorrow for craft day, if that is okay? I want someone to remember me here once I leave."

I glanced over at the gang and then at Noah as I tried to contain my tears. I'd worried about what harm telling Sarah she'd be going into foster care would do. I had at least allowed her time to process the loss of her parents before I explained to her what would happen when the time came.

"Yes, bring it with you. We are donating to a few families this year," I said, swallowing hard. "And you'll always be remembered here." I smiled softly as I placed my hand on top of her head.

"Ready to go, Sarah?" Gracie asked, coming over to the table.

Sarah looked up at me and held out the basket, which I took as I smiled at her. "Can I go?"

"Of course, we will be over in a minute," I said, as she wrapped her arms around my waist, hugging me.

We all watched her and Gracie walk across the park to the gazebo in silence.

"Have you thought about putting in an adoption application?" Trinity questioned quietly.

I nodded. "I have, but I already know that they won't even consider me. Single mom. I've seen this before; they want a family situation for a child like Sarah."

"No harm in trying though," Thomas added. "Never know what they will decide. Maybe if they see how happy she is with you, it may tip the scales in your favor."

I nodded, knowing full well he was right, but I didn't want to get my hopes up.

"It's all about finding the most stable location for her," Noah said. "If you are the one providing that, then the power lies with you. They may watch to see how things go with you before they decide. It's worth it to put an application in." Noah placed his hand on my back.

"What do you say we all head back over to the diner

after the carols and have some coffee and cake?" Peggy asked, coming up beside me, Ethan and Noah behind her.

"I'm down for that," Noah agreed. "Do you have any of that double fudge cake, Brooke?"

"I think I can find one somewhere over there." She giggled.

"Perfect, what do you say, Mindi, want to join me?" Noah asked.

It sounded wonderful, but I was tired and feeling a little down, especially after seeing how sad Sarah was. I hated that she'd be leaving the only home she'd ever known.

"I'd love to, but I think after we do the carols, I'm going to head home and get Sarah tucked into bed," I answered. "I'm tired, and I have to be up early to go over the receipts from the tree farm before I open up tomorrow morning. Otherwise, it's going to get out of hand."

"Oh, okay then."

"You'll still join us though, right, Noah?" Ethan asked.

"Wouldn't miss it," he said, grabbing the large pot Brooke had used to put the hot chocolate in.

Sarah and I meandered through the park, admiring the lights as we made our way to the car. I felt so empty inside for most of the night. There were so many things I was facing at the moment, and I didn't have a clue how I was supposed to feel about any of them.

Sarah climbed into the front seat of my car, while I pulled the snow brush from the back seat and cleared the windows, then threw it back inside, hoping into the front seat. I shoved the key into the ignition and turned it, my car making a funny sputtering sound. I tried it again, and once again, the same thing happened.

"That doesn't sound very good," Sarah said, looking over at me.

"No, it doesn't," I said, once again trying to start the car only to have the same thing happen.

I closed my eyes. The last thing I needed on top of saving for the repairs on the Potts tree farm truck was my car to act up. I turned the key again, listening to the same sputtering sound it had let out before.

"Oh, come on...don't do this," I cried, trying again, this time holding my breath as if it were going to make a difference.

When the car failed to turn over, I rested my forehead against the steering wheel and let out a small scream.

"It's okay," Sarah said, patting my shoulder.

"Oh, dear, I wish that were true," I whispered as I

looked over at The Crispy Biscuit. We needed a ride home, and I had no choice but to ask for one.

"Come on, put your mitts back on." I sighed, opening the car door, waiting for Sarah to come around and join me.

"Where are we going?"

"To see if someone can give us a ride home."

"Maybe Noah could," she said, smiling up at me.

"I don't think it has to be Noah. Ethan and Peggy could give us a lift."

"No, I think Noah should. He's nice."

"He is nice," I said, taking her hand in mine and smiling down.

"He's the one from the letters, isn't he?" she asked, looking up at me.

"How did you know that?" I questioned.

She shrugged. "He told me he used to date you."

"He did, did he? When did he tell you that?"

"Yesterday, when we were decorating the cookies. He also told me he thinks you're pretty."

"What else did the two of you talk about?" I questioned as we made our way down the street.

"My mom and dad. He told me he knew them. He's really easy to talk to, just like you."

"Let's go," I said, taking her hand as we crossed the street.

"I saw you guys skating in the park."

"Yes, we used to skate when we were younger."

"Do you think the two of you might date?"

"Oh, Sarah, where are these questions coming from?"

Sarah shrugged. "I don't know; you just seemed happy tonight."

"You know me; I love this time of year, and I'm always happy."

"That is true," Sarah said, picking up the pace to catch up to me, as we stopped in front of The Crispy Biscuit and pulled the door open to be greeted by laughter.

I stepped inside to see Noah look over at me.

"Mindi, what is it?" he questioned, getting up from the table as the rest of my friends went on talking and laughing.

"My car won't start," I said, letting out a sigh.

"Need a ride?" he questioned.

Before I could say anything, Sarah answered for us.

"Can you drive us home?"

Noah looked at me and smiled.

"It doesn't have to be you," I said, bumping Sarah's shoulder.

Noah looked down at Sarah and winked. "If you need a ride, I don't mind."

I glanced out the window and over at my car and then looked back at Noah. "You sure you don't mind?" I asked.

He shook his head. "No, I don't mind. Why don't you

come sit for a bit, have a coffee and some cake. We will get going shortly."

"We really should—"

"Yay! Coffee and cake!" Sarah shouted, running on over to the table where everyone was sitting.

"Come on," he urged.

I smiled softly as he gently guided us over to the table where Trinity immediately made room for us both to sit down, and Brooke grabbed a mug full of coffee and placed it down in front of me while grabbing a hot cider for Sarah.

I hadn't planned on being so late, but conversation with good friends goes that way. It was almost midnight when Noah pulled into the driveway and drove down to the house, where he stopped his truck.

"Thanks," I said, looking over at him.

"My pleasure. Looks like the little lady is sound asleep."

I glanced over my shoulder into the backseat to see Sarah lying across the backseat, asleep.

"Didn't she tell us she wasn't tired when we left?" I giggled.

"She did. Did you want some help to get her inside?"

I let out a sigh. Sarah was very close to my full height for being twelve, and I knew there was no way I'd be able to pick her up.

"Do you mind?" I questioned.

Noah shook his head and cut the engine of his truck, then climbed out of the front seat while I gathered my things and dug for my keys. He followed me up the front steps, Sarah in his arms while I opened the door.

I shut the door behind him and led the way down to Sarah's room, where he placed her down on the bed.

"Give me a couple of minutes," I said gently, removing her coat.

Once I'd gotten her coat and hat off, I covered her up and then made my way into the living room, where I found Noah standing looking around the room.

"You still have the stand?"

"Sure do. Still working the trees too."

"I know; I got a flyer. It was nice to see your dad actually made this work. How are your parents?"

"Mom passed away four years ago, and Dad sadly went just before Christmas the year before last."

"I'm sorry, I didn't know."

"I know. What about yours?"

"Mom passed a few years back, and Dad is out at that retirement community. He has dementia. The last time I was out there he didn't remember me."

"Oh, Noah, I'm sorry to hear that."

Noah nodded, looking around the house. "It still looks the same," he said as I stood beside him.

"What does?"

"This house, your old room," he said, turning to face me. "It brings back all these memories."

"I know. Not much changes around here." I smiled.

"Some things do, but not much," Noah said, meeting my eyes. Even with that long-lost look in them, they were still gorgeous. It was all I could do to tear mine away from his.

"It's late. I have to be up early to go over the sales from the trees today."

"Yeah, gosh, I should get going. About the car—"

"Don't worry about it, I'll get out to town later tomorrow and get it looked after."

"You're sure? I can always meet you and take a look at it."

"I'm sure. No worries. Have a good night."

"So you know, I had a fantastic time tonight," he whispered, placing his hand on the small of my back.

"So did I. It was like old times."

Noah stepped out the front door and turned to look at me. As our eyes met, it felt as if everything fell away. We stood there, staring into one another's eyes, and slowly we moved toward one another until our lips touched. It felt like I'd been holding my breath forever, but when his lips finally met mine, my soul quieted. The upset, the pain, the wondering all finally quieted as he kissed me.

The moment our lips parted, the silence went away and things got loud again. He looked at me, and I at him. I knew full well what that kiss meant, and in those moments, I felt the walls I'd built up come crashing down. No one had kissed me that way but him. My heart still belonged to him, which made me question if it hadn't always.

"Good night," I whispered.

"Night."

I watched him walk down my front porch steps and climb into his truck. Once he drove away, I went back inside and shut the door.

Noah

"I can't thank you enough for coming by," I said to Zach as he approached carrying a set of spark plugs and oil.

"Ah not a problem, gets me out of hanging garland." He laughed.

"At this rate, Iris is going to kill me when she sees me. I've come to town and am taking you away from doing all the things she needs done." I chuckled, taking the spark plugs from the bag.

"Nah, she'll just make you help me. Does Mindi know you're here working on the car?"

"No, when I got back home last night from dropping her off, I found her car key on the floor of my truck. It must have fallen off her keychain when she pulled her house keys from her purse. She had a lot to do out at the house and told me she couldn't get here until later today, so I figured I'd just come on down and see if I could fix it."

"You're sure it's the plugs?"

I couldn't help but laugh. "Oh, it's the plugs. They look like they haven't been changed since I left for deployment ten years ago."

"Oh man, all right then, let's get to it."

We got to work right away, and within an hour, Mindi's car was sitting in the lot running. I glanced down at my watch, surprised it was only a little past nine.

"I'll give you a lift back to the house before I take the car out to Mindi. That way you can help Iris with the garland."

"Actually, perhaps I'll follow you out. Iris also wanted me to get the trees today anyway, and by the time we get out there, the stand should be open."

"Here, take my truck. That way, you can give me a lift back into town," I said, throwing him the keys.

"Sounds good to me," Zach said, catching them.

I was surprised to see that Mindi's small parking lot in front of her home was full when we arrived, and people were buzzing around, grabbing their trees. Zach and I parked, and while I made my way to the front door, Zach headed over to the lot.

"Noah!" Sarah exclaimed when she opened the door.

"Hey, Sarah! Is Mindi here?"

Sarah nodded, and then I heard Mindi's frustrated voice inside.

"She's in the living room on the phone. She's upset."

"Oh, how come?" I asked, stepping inside while Sarah closed the front door.

"Gabe and Connor can't deliver the trees to the people in town today. Apparently, they had a farm emergency."

I glanced around the corner to see Mindi pacing back and forth as she spoke on the phone. I lifted my hand and waved to her only to have her ignore me, turn around, and go back to her conversation.

"See what I mean?" Sarah said, pulling the cat she held closer to her. "Bad mood."

"Who's this?" I questioned, patting the cat on the head.

"Sparkles, Mindi's cat. She is my best friend."

"Hi, Sparkles. Don't the two of you worry, I'll help Mindi," I said, winking at Sarah.

I stepped out of my snowy boots and made my way over to where Mindi stood looking down at the table.

"Good morning," I greeted, stepping up beside Mindi.

"Is it? I hadn't noticed." She sighed.

"It is," I said, pulling her car key from my pocket and holding it out to her.

"What?" she said, raising her glassy eyes to mine.

"You dropped your car key in my truck last night."

"I did?" she asked, grabbing her keychain.

"I looked at your car this morning too. You shouldn't ignore your spark plugs," I whispered, watching as a smile slowly crept onto her face.

"That's what was wrong?" she questioned.

"That's all. It fired up right away the moment I changed them. I also put some oil in there too; it was a little low. You'll need to get it in for service soon, but you'll be fine for a bit, at least until after Christmas."

"Thank you," she said immediately, wrapping her arms around me in a tight hug.

"No need to thank me. Now, what else is going on? Sarah said something about deliveries."

"Yeah, Gabe Bentley and Connor Darling, they help each year since the Potts Tree Farm truck went down, but this morning, there was an emergency, and they both needed to tend to it. So, I'm down for deliveries on one of the busiest weekends of the holiday season." She sighed.

"Well, it looks like a holiday angel is looking over your shoulder. I just happen to have my truck outside, and Zach is here with me. I think between the two of us, we could probably get the trees delivered."

"No, I couldn't ask you to do that after you fixed—"

I shook my head and reached out, placing both of my hands on her shoulders, stopping her from continuing.

"You aren't asking, I'm offering. Now, could I get the list of deliveries?"

She studied me for a moment and then grabbed the list off the table, handing it to me.

"Now, some of these can wait—"

"No, they can't. They are due to be delivered today, and we will get them done. I won't have people being disappointed at this time of year. I'll have Zach call Iris and explain, and between the two of us, we will get them all delivered." I winked.

I went to head back to the door when I felt Mindi grab hold of my arm, stopping me. I turned and looked at her to see a soft smile spread across her face.

"Thank you," she whispered.

"My pleasure."

I made my way past Sarah, who stood there with a smile on her face.

"See, I told you." I winked at her as I walked to the door, shoved my feet into my boots, and left the house to find Zach.

It was well past seven when I dropped Zach off at home and took a drive back out to see Mindi. My stomach let out a rumble as I pulled my truck up to the house and cut the engine. We hadn't stopped all day and had made many trips back and forth, finishing just an hour ago. I was just about to the steps when the front door opened and Sarah stepped outside.

"Hey, Noah!" She waved.

"Hey, kiddo."

"Did you get all the trees delivered?" she questioned, excitement in her voice.

"We sure did. Did you have any doubts?"

"Not one. I knew you'd do it. Come inside, we are just about to eat. You can stay for dinner," she said, leading the way inside.

"Oh, no, that isn't necessary. I'm not intruding. I just want to let Mindi know all the trees were delivered and then I'll be on my way."

Instantly, I noticed Sarah's smile vanish, and she let out a tiny sigh after she called to Mindi.

"What is it, Sarah?" she asked, coming around the corner, noticing me standing there. "Oh, hey, Noah."

"Hey, they are all delivered," I said, passing her the paper she'd given me that contained all the addresses.

She took the paper from me and looked down at it, tears coming to her eyes. "I don't know how to thank you," she said.

"A thank you isn't necessary. It was my pleasure."

"If you want to thank him, he could stay for dinner

and help decorate the tree later," I heard Sarah whisper, which I ignored.

"Anyway, if you need any more help here, just let me know," I said, turning to leave. "I'd be happy to look at the old truck too, if you'd like."

"That's not necessary, but thank you."

"Ask him," I heard Sarah whisper again.

"You know, why don't you stay for dinner? You're probably freezing, and hungry."

"Oh no, I don't want to impose."

It was then Sarah jumped up and ran over to us, grabbing hold of my arm, stopping me from opening the door.

"You're not imposing. Come on, we're having roast beef, and we are going to decorate the tree tonight," she said, grabbing my arm and pulling me inside.

"Looks like you're staying." Mindi laughed.

"I think so." I chuckled, shrugged out of my coat, which Sarah took and shoved into the closet, and without hesitation led me over to the table where she quickly grabbed another place setting from the cupboard.

"Well, what do you think?" Mindi asked as the three of us stood in front of the decorated tree.

"We need the topper!" Sarah shouted, running over to the table and bringing over the angel. "It's so pretty."

"That it is," Mindi said with a soft smile on her face but a faraway look in her eye. "Do you remember this?" she questioned, looking up at me.

I turned to see the angel Sarah held in her hands.

"You still have that?" I questioned.

"I do. It's been at the top of my tree every year," Mindi answered.

"Was it from your mom?" Sarah asked, placing the angel on the couch and grabbing the step stool.

The room was quiet as both Mindi and I looked at one another.

"Can I put it on the tree?" Sarah questioned, setting up the stool at the base of the tree.

"I'll help you," I said, grabbing the angel and waiting while Sarah carefully climbed up the stool, while both Mindi and I held her to make sure she didn't fall.

Sarah placed the angel on top and then carefully climbed back down and looked up at the tree.

"Well, the angel—did it come from your mom and dad?" she questioned again.

Mindi smiled, pulling her against her. "No, that angel came from Noah," she answered softly, looking at me.

"Really?"

I nodded. "Really."

"You gave me that the Christmas before you were

deployed. When we agreed to move in together. We started looking for a place, and then you were sent to Afghanistan and..."

"Really?" Sarah questioned.

"Yep...really," I muttered, noticing the faraway look in her eyes.

"Anyway, Sarah, why don't you go make the popcorn and bring in three sodas for the movie while Noah and I tidy up in here."

"Got it! Are we watching—"

"Yes! Of course, we are going to watch *The Grinch*," Mindi said, smiling as we both watched Sarah run into the kitchen.

Mindi pulled the door closed to Sarah's room and sat down beside me. She began loading the empty soda tins and bowls onto the tray that sat on the table.

"Well, did you enjoy?" she questioned.

"I did. This actually feels like a real Christmas this year."

"I'm glad."

"I still can't believe you kept that angel," I said, looking up at the tree and then over to her.

"I couldn't get rid of it. It came from you," she said, meeting my eyes.

With the quietness of *Silent Night* playing on the TV, I slowly leaned forward and pressed my lips against hers. I could feel the tension in her body go, and a slow-building fire inside of mine ignite.

"I can't believe you came back," she murmured before she wrapped her arms around me and kissed me harder.

I guided her to straddle my lap and pulled her against me, my tongue washing through her mouth. She tasted exactly as I remembered, and as I continued kissing her, she let out a soft moan, running her fingers up the back of my head and into my hair.

I could feel myself growing hard when she broke the kiss and looked at me. Her eyes were dark and heavy, like she wanted to carry this on to the next level, but I wasn't ready.

"I should go," I whispered. "It's late, and I don't want to make a mistake by taking things too far."

"I know, neither do I."

She looked at me, running her fingers through my hair again, and then leaned down and kissed my lips before getting off my lap and walking me to the door where we kissed goodbye.

Mindi

Ten Days before Christmas

Things were finally coming together at the Community Center, and with Ethan's help, we worked together to set up Noah's office. So far he'd been with us a full week and already had a full schedule. I'd gotten lucky to get Sarah in to talk to him today.

I glanced at my watch as I made my way down the hall to his office and stopped just outside the door, peeking in the window to see them sitting on the couch talking away. I had feared she'd never open up and that when the time came for her to be moved to her new family that she'd struggle. I wanted to give her the best chance of success at settling in with whomever they placed her with, and I'd done all that I could to help. Noah was the next logical step. I was surprised to see that she was talking his ear off and even laughing.

I knocked on the door, wishing I didn't need to interrupt, and popped my head into Noah's new office.

"Hey, Mindi, we were just finishing up," Noah said, smiling.

"How did it go?" I questioned, looking at Sarah.

"Good."

"Great. Well, are you just about ready to head on over to see Gracie?" I questioned.

"Yes! I'm so excited to sleep over, and if I go now, that means you can head out on your date," Sarah said, batting her eyelashes at me and giggling.

Sarah asked me last week if she could sleep over at Gracie's this week, and so we called and spoken to Iris and made a plan. Shortly after my phone call with Iris, I invited Noah for dinner, which he'd quickly accepted.

"Alright, miss, that is enough." I laughed as she puckered her lips and sent kisses into the air. "Where is that coming from?"

Sarah shrugged and then laughed as she took off out of the room and headed to my office to grab her things.

I stood there watching as Noah made a couple of notes and then tucked a file into the pile on his desk before looking up at me.

"Everything go okay?" I asked.

"Yep, went fine. We worked through a lot today," Noah said, getting up from where he sat and moving to his desk. "You don't need to worry about her. She is going to be fine."

"I'm glad, but I'll always worry."

Noah looked up at me and smiled. "I know. It wouldn't be like you if you didn't." He said, coming over to me, placing a kiss on my lips. "So, shall I bring dessert tonight?"

"That would be nice. I am going to run her over to Zach and Iris's and then head on out and get the stand closed down."

"Sounds good. I will see you about six then?" he questioned, glancing at his watch.

"Six works."

"Okay, see you then. Ready, kiddo?" I questioned as Sarah stopped in the doorway watching the both of us, bags in her hands.

"Ready." She smiled. "Could we stop at The Crispy Biscuit and get some treats for Gracie and I?" she asked, looking up at me.

"Well, what about the boys, Dylan and Noah? Should we get something for them too?"

"I guess."

"You guess? I think we should. I also think that we should get something for Iris and Zach as well, okay?"

"Okay, have fun on your date," Sarah said, waving to Noah.

"Have fun at your sleepover." He winked at Sarah and then winked at me as we turned to leave.

"You awake?" I heard Noah ask quietly.

I opened my eyes to see the credits rolling on the TV, my head rested on his shoulder.

"Hmmm, yes," I said, sitting up a little and looking at Noah with sleepy eyes.

We'd had a nice quiet dinner, talking about the past and catching one another up on all that we'd been through over the years. After, Noah built a fire while I cleaned up the dishes and put things away. Then, we settled down together, curled up on the couch with a couple of blankets, and watched a movie.

"Wow, it's late. I didn't realize the time. I guess I should get home," he said, placing his hand on my thigh and smiling gently.

The conversation between us had flowed as easily as it always had, but I knew there were still a lot of unsaid words between us, and now the thought of him leaving was causing a very heavy feeling inside of me. He got up from where he was sitting and made his way over to the front hall closet as I came up behind him.

"Thank you for dinner. It was wonderful," he said, pushing a strand of hair behind my ears before stopping to look me in the eyes.

"You're welcome. I'm glad you enjoyed."

He threw his coat on and then leaned forward and pressed his lips to mine. I closed my eyes, allowing myself to let go and just let the warm feeling awaken me.

"Night, Mindi," he whispered and opened the door, stepping out into the snowy night air.

"Night."

I watched him walk down the stairs toward his truck and then went back inside and shut the door. As I stood there with my back pressed to the door, I realized I didn't want him to leave; I wanted him to stay, but I couldn't move. It was rare for me to have the house to myself, and I knew I needed to open the door, call out to him and tell him to come back inside, but I just stood there, leaning against the door. I heard his engine start and then trail off into the night.

I made my way into the living room, stopping after only a few steps. I really didn't want him to leave. I turned around and made my way back to the door, pulling it open. I was shocked to see Noah standing there, and before I could say anything, he'd wrapped his arms around me, kissing me hard.

He backed me into the house, closing the door behind him, then shrugged out of his jacket as we continued to kiss.

"I couldn't leave," he whispered. "Not this time."

My hands found the buttons of his shirt, unbuttoning one at a time, finally shoving the material off his shoulders. He broke our kiss only to lift my shirt up and over my head, dropping it to the floor where his lay. Then he pulled me against his warm chest, his hands running down my body, cupping my ass as he pulled me closer.

"Is it wrong that I've wanted you all this time?" he murmured. "That I still want you?"

My body heated as he kissed the side of my neck, his one hand now resting gently on my cheek as his other snaked through my hair, gently tugging it as his lips met mine again.

"I still want you to." I closed my eyes, relishing the feel of his lips against my skin.

I couldn't help but let out a quiet moan as his tongue washed through my mouth as his hands ran over my back. He played with the clasp on my bra, my nipples hardening as the material fell away. He looked down into my eyes as he gently removed it, dropping it to the pile that lay at our feet, before he took my breasts in his hands, cupping them, running his thumbs over my nipples.

"I want you," he murmured, pulling me against his bare chest, kissing me hard.

"I want you too," I whispered, tugging on his jeans to follow me down the hall where we entered my bedroom and closed the door.

Noah

I woke in the middle of the night, forgetting where I was, until I felt the bed move and I looked over to see Mindi sound asleep. I watched her for a while, remembering the feel of her fingers digging into my back as she arched her back off the mattress, crying out as she came. As I looked at her, sleeping peacefully, and all I wanted to do was see her face again as she cried out my name.

Half an hour later, I carefully slipped out of the bed to use the washroom and get a drink of water.

I quietly made my way through the house and back into the bedroom and was about to place the glass on the bedside table when something caught my eye. I blinked a couple of times to make sure I wasn't seeing things and then slowly set the glass down. I reached up and grabbed a card that sat on her nightstand. As I looked at it, my heart stopped. Then I opened the card, and in the few seconds that it took for me to read the first few words, my world stopped. I sat down on the edge of the bed, reading and re-reading the card.

"Good morning," I heard Mindi say behind me.

I didn't know how long I'd been sitting on the edge of the bed, but when I tore my eyes from the card, light streamed in through the windows. My mind was racing and my chest was tight as I looked down at the front of that card again. All these years, all the wondering I'd done, the fucking heartbreak I'd gone through, and now I finally had my answer. This had to be some sort of cruel joke.

"Good morning, silly." She giggled.

I felt the bed move, but the moment I felt her hands on my shoulders, I pulled away and got up.

"Noah is...is something wrong?"

I ran my fingers through my messy hair and fought to breathe as I paced back and forth. I really should have just left when I found it, but I'd been paralyzed by shock. I probably should have asked her about this when we first sat down, but I'd been afraid of the answer, but now I had it.

"Noah? What is wrong?" she asked, sitting on her knees now in the center of the bed, the blankets wrapped around her naked body.

I studied her a moment, and then I held up the card.

The way the smile fell away from her lips when she

saw what was in my hands, the way her eyes studied the card said it all. She didn't need to explain anything, but still I wanted to hear it from her. I wanted to hear it from her she'd decided against marrying me. It was as if I wanted to punish myself all over again.

"So...you got it?" I said, my voice cracking as the words left my lips.

"Noah, please let me explain," she said, scrambling off the bed and throwing a T-shirt over her head.

"Explain..." I huffed, looking down at that card again and then dropping it on top of the dresser.

"Yes, let me explain."

"Explain what? That it was just easier not to respond than to tell me you didn't want to marry me?"

"I just got the card a few weeks ago; it got lost. If you give me a minute, I will find the bag it came in, and the envelope. The address got smudged."

I looked at the card and then over at her, frantically searching through a pile of papers she had on the other bedside table.

"You know, it was hard enough having to ask you the biggest question of my life inside of a damn card."

She stopped rustling through the pile of papers and looked at me.

"I would never get to see your initial reaction to my question. I'd never get to see the surprise or the joy or the fear in your eyes. I'd never get to hear the yes, or hug and kiss you afterward. I was a million miles away in some hell-hole country, waiting, praying, begging that you'd say yes. Instead, I never heard a word from you again. It tore my heart out."

"I swear to you, Noah, if you just give me a minute to think..." she said, her hands covering her face. "I can show you..." she said, tears coming to her eyes.

I took another look at the card. It was perfect—not a tear, not a drop of dirt, nothing. I picked it up, opened it, looking for any signs of wear and tear, but there was nothing.

"Just stop, okay. It doesn't matter. That card is in perfect shape, like you just pulled it from a box. It's been ten years. If that card had gotten lost, it would be a mangled mess by now. Instead, it's near fucking perfect."

I dropped it back down on the table and looked over at her, still frantically searching through the pile once again. That was when I noticed the box of letters. I picked up the top one and recognized my handwriting on the envelope. Seeing the letters and the card together told me the only thing I needed to know. I grabbed my shirt, threw it over my head, and took off out of the bedroom.

"Noah, please, just look!" Mindi yelled. "The envelope, it's all smudged, and here is the bag—"

She grabbed my arm, pulling on me, trying to get me to turn around, but I refused. I slipped my feet into my boots, grabbed my jacket, and pulled the front door open.

"Noah, please....just let me show you..."

"You know what, I should have thought about this before, but I can't do this with you."

"You can't do what?" she cried, stopping at the top of the stairs.

"This, us. I thought you were the same person I left all those years ago. I wanted to ask you about the card. I really wanted to believe it had just gotten lost. At least that was what I told myself. I wanted to believe that you'd not walk away from me the way you did."

"I didn't. I wrote to you every week for an entire year," she cried.

"Mindi, please, it's alright. The girl I know never would have left me hanging. She'd have gone to the ends of the earth to try to get in touch with me. She'd have written, she'd have answered even if she didn't want to marry me. I'd like to believe she'd have let me down gently. Instead, now, my naivety has allowed me to be gutted once again."

Tears filled her eyes as she stood on those stairs, clutching an envelope and plastic bag in her hand. I couldn't stay and watch it. I didn't say another word. I grabbed the handle of the car door and pulled it open. I cranked the key, fired the engine, and took off down the driveway.

Two Days Later

Exhaustion filled me as I climbed the steps up to the door of the Willow Valley Bed and Breakfast. I raised my arm and knocked on the door, waiting for someone to answer. I was about to knock again when the door opened and Iris stood there grinning.

"Noah! Welcome."

"Hey, Iris."

"What do we owe for this pleasant surprise? How are you? You know you never have to knock." She smiled, stepping aside to let me inside.

"I know. I just didn't want to intrude."

"Nonsense, you are like family. Come on in. I just made some fresh cookies, and there is leftover breakfast if you'd like a plate. You know I always make too much, especially when we aren't full."

"Sounds great. I could use a little food," I said, patting my grumbling stomach.

I had been planning on calling Zach and asking him to meet me over at The Crispy Biscuit, but I knew Mindi would more than likely be there before heading to the community center this morning. I'd called in last night after I knew she'd left. Right now, she was the last person I wanted to run into. I'd spent most of the nights following the night at her place tossing and turning, thinking about that card and the months of agonizing I'd done over it when I'd been younger.

I followed Iris into the kitchen, where her two boys, Noah and Dylan, were just finishing up their juice.

"Hey, boys!" I said, ruffling their hair as I sat down beside them.

"Hey, Noah," they both said right before shoving the last bite of French toast into their mouths.

Iris placed a plate of French toast down in front of me and then grabbed the bottle of syrup from the opposite end of the table for me. "I'll just warm up a couple of sausage, and here is a fresh cup of coffee too." She winked.

"Thank you." I smiled, adding some syrup to my plate and taking a bite. "Good as always," I added.

I dug into the French toast for another bite, not realizing just how hungry I was.

"Damn right it is. This woman makes the best French toast," I heard Zach say as he walked into the kitchen and came over, holding his hand out for me to shake.

"Hey, man. How's things?" I questioned, sitting back down as Zach sat across from me, while Iris placed a cup of coffee in front of him.

"Good, good. Did that painter contact you?" he questioned.

I shook my head. I really hadn't checked my messages

or had time to even think about the painter reference I'd asked for.

"I'll get back on her. She's been swamped," Zach added.

"No need, I'm not sure how much longer I'll be staying in Willow Valley," I admitted.

Zach and Iris both stopped and looked at me, questions in their eyes.

"What? Are you serious?" Zach asked. "You seemed thrilled the other night." He winked.

I'd told Zach all about Mindi and me, and I'd shared how excited I was that I might have found her again.

"I'm afraid so," I said, taking another bite of my breakfast.

"May I ask why?" Zach questioned. "We'd hate to see you leave so soon after just getting settled into that beautiful house."

"This doesn't have something to do with Mindi, does it?" Iris asked, bringing over a couple of sausages and placing them on my plate.

"Why?"

"Oh, no reason. She just didn't seem herself when she picked Sarah up this morning."

"I thought Sarah was only staying for one night?" I asked, swallowing hard.

"That was the plan, but Mindi called me on Saturday morning and asked me if it was okay if she stayed another night. Said something to me about not feeling very well, and she was adamant she didn't want to talk about it, and when I offered to bring her over some homemade chicken soup, she refused, telling me she'd be alright."

As Iris looked at me, I suddenly felt like a bit of a child. I'd played over everything in my head for the past two days, and I realized I really hadn't let her get a word in edgewise that morning. I'd never allowed her to explain. When I saw that card again, and my writing inside, it had taken me right back to the moment I'd dropped it in the mail. I could remember exactly how I'd felt dropping it into the bin, the moment of panic after I'd let the card go and it had dropped to the bottom with no hope of getting it back.

"It's a long story," I said, somewhat chuckling.

Iris dropped the cloth she'd been cleaning the counters with into the sink of water, grabbed her mug of coffee, and came over to sit beside Zach.

"We have time." She winked, both of them turning their attention to me.

I took my time explaining and sharing with them everything up to this exact point, and took a cookie off the plate in the center of the table while I waited for them to respond. Both of them sat there, glancing at one another, a little sly smile on both their lips when I stopped talking, and then they both turned and looked at me.

"We know you are hurting. It's clear. Though I think

you need to give her a chance to explain," Iris said. "I mean, you are a counselor. You know the importance of allowing someone time to explain their side, but you stopped her before she had the chance."

Iris had hit the nail on the head. I was exactly that, and I knew the importance. Only it seemed different when you were the one in the middle of the conflict. It was easier to cast the blame and run, not allowing the other person to voice their side and risk being hurt by the truth.

"What if what I believe is true? That she got the card and chose not to respond?" I questioned.

"Well, I think then you have a right to know. However, without knowing Mindi well, I know what her heart is like, and I know she'd not do anything to anyone just to intentionally hurt them," Iris said, resting her hand under her chin and looking at Zach. "What do you think?" she questioned.

"I agree. I think maybe you need to give it some time. Digest what your beliefs are, and once you have done that and calmed down and are ready to be open enough to listen, and I really stress that part, then approach her. Obviously, the shock of seeing that card again was what drove you to act the way you did. You weren't expecting to see the card. Instead, you were maybe ready to take the relationship you once had and see if there was anything still there. I think you need to give her a chance to really explain and share with you, not railroad her."

"Oh God, I did that, didn't I?" I said, running my hands over my face.

"I'm afraid so," Zach added while Iris nodded.

"I'm a horrible person," I said, taking a sip of my coffee and shoving another cookie into my mouth.

"No, you are human," Iris said, getting up from her chair just as Grace came into the kitchen, her head hung low.

"Hey, Gracie," I said.

Zach turned and looked at his daughter and then tapped his knee. "What is it, pumpkin?" he questioned.

Grace climbed up onto his knee while Iris brought over a glass of milk and handed her a cookie.

"I'm just sad."

"Why?" Iris questioned, looking to me and then back to Grace.

"Because Sarah is going to be leaving. She didn't want you to know, or for Mindi to know, but she was crying last night."

Iris patted Gracie's head as she buried her face in her father's shoulder. Zach looked over at me and hugged his daughter.

"Why?"

"She wants to stay with Mindi. Noah, can you help her?" Gracie asked, looking over at me with her huge brown eyes.

"Oh, sweetie, I don't think Noah can do anything for

her, but don't be sad for her," Iris said. "She's going to find a new home."

"I know, but it won't be here." She pouted.

Iris looked at me and smiled softly. "Gracie and Sarah became great friends over the summer."

"Well, you can still be friends. Distance doesn't stop that," I said.

"Please, there must be something you can do for her."

"I'm sorry, sweetheart, but it's not up to me," I said, looking at both Zach and Iris.

"Gracie, why don't you take your milk and cookies and go watch some TV?" Iris said, grabbing her a small glass of milk.

"Fine." She sighed, then grabbed her glass of milk and hopped off her father's lap and took off toward the sitting room, leaving the three of us in the kitchen once again.

"Grace has been hinting that we should take Sarah in," Iris told me.

"Ah, I see," I answered.

"She thinks it's that easy. We've tried explaining things to her, but, well, she's eleven."

"Yep, we have to love how children think," Zach added.

"Looks like we all have things we wish were easy to contend with. I'm gonna get out of your hair. Laundry and house chores call."

"How about you come for dinner tomorrow night?

Iris is making a large roast, and we only have one overnight guest this week, so there will be plenty."

I looked at them, thankful to both of them for making me feel so welcome.

"Since I can't say no to that invite, I'll see you both then," I said, getting up and placing a kiss on Iris's cheek before shaking hands with Zach.

Mindi

I sat in my small office at the community center staring out the window. Sarah had gone over to see Gracie for another sleepover after she'd had her appointment with Noah.

I took a sip of tea and stared at the paper application in front of me. I had to be out of my mind thinking that they'd ever look at me as a viable option for Sarah. I picked up my pen and slowly began filling out the top section when I heard a knock on my door.

"We're finished. Going to head out now, unless there is something else you need," Ethan said, stepping into my office.

I looked up and saw Noah in the hallway, his back to me. He hadn't looked at me since the morning he'd left, which stung more than I wanted to admit.

"I'm good. Have a good night." I sighed.

"Everything alright?" Ethan asked with a slight frown on his face.

"Fine. See you later this week."

Ethan nodded and then turned to leave but stopped again. "Oh, before I forget, you are still coming for dinner tonight, right?"

I let out a deep sigh, debating telling him I wasn't coming, then thought about the broccoli casserole I'd worked hard to make that morning and changed my mind.

"I'll be there," I answered.

"Good, we will see you then."

I watched as Ethan turned toward the exit door, followed by Noah, who I'd have thought would at least wave, or poke his head in and tell me how things went with Sarah, but there was nothing. Again, he didn't even look in my direction. It was as if I didn't exist. He hadn't said a word to me the entire week.

I looked down at the paperwork in front of me. I didn't know what I was even thinking when I printed the adoption application off the website to keep Sarah with me. Yet, here it sat. I took my time, thinking through each of my answers before I wrote a word.

When I had finished, and I was confident with every-thing I'd written, I flipped the page. My heart sank as I read the next part. They wanted references — five of them.

They were specific—not only character references, but one of them had to be from the military, which wasn't a problem. Ethan had agreed, but the other was going to be difficult. They wanted a reference from a therapist, one who knew me, and one who had talked to Sarah, one who would look at the situation without bias.

There was absolutely no way I could ever ask Noah to be a reference now. He wouldn't even look at me. Hell, we'd slept together, and he wouldn't even give me a chance to explain what he's seen.

My heart sank, yet I calmly filled each one of them out, then slipped the pages into my fax machine and sent them off, praying that I'd hear something before Christmas.

The moment the fax had gone through, I grabbed my bag and took off over to Ethan and Peggy's for dinner.

I pulled into the driveway at Ethan and Peggy's house and slid my car in behind Trinity's, cutting the engine. I looked at the house, taking a glimpse at the tree that was lit in the large front window, and softly smiled.

This really was my favorite time of year, but this year I'd struggled to find some sort of Christmas spirit. I'd spent most of the week hiding out at home, trying hard to put Noah to the back of my mind. Seeing his face as he stared at that card that morning, after the feelings I'd just experienced with him the night before, had haunted my dreams.

I gathered my purse and the broccoli casserole and climbed out of the car, careful not to slip on the ice, and made my way over to the door. I was just about to knock when the door opened and Ethan stood there with a smile on his face.

"Hey, Mindi, come on in," he said, reaching for the casserole dish I was carrying.

"Thanks," I said, stepping inside and placing my purse on the hook followed by my coat.

"Hey, Mindi," I heard from inside the house. "Come on in, grab a drink and join us."

I looked at Ethan, slipped my shoes off, and then followed him into the kitchen.

"How are you doing?" he asked, looking at me with concern as he poured some punch into a cup for me.

Ethan knew something had happened between Noah and me, but I didn't tell him the entire story.

"You okay, kid?" he questioned as he slipped the casserole I'd brought into the oven to warm.

"I'm not sure," I muttered, my vision blurring just as Peggy, Trinity, and Thomas came into the kitchen.

"Mindi, sweetheart, what is it?" Peggy asked, coming straight over and wrapping her arms around me.

"Oh, you know, just life." I sniffled, hugging her back.

"Is it Sarah?" Trinity asked.

"Yes and no," I said, grabbing a napkin and dabbing my eyes. "I put my application in tonight. That was what I was working on when you stopped by my office."

"That's wonderful," Thomas said, sitting down beside Trinity.

"Yes, but that shouldn't bring on the tears."

"It shouldn't, but it is. There is no way I'll get custody of her. The application wanted five references."

"My dear, certainly we can find another one."

"Absolutely, anyone in this community would stand up and recommend you," Ethan added.

"That's the problem. They don't want just anyone. They want an approved counselor."

I watched as they looked at one another and then turned to me.

"Mindi, do you forget you have a military-approved counselor working for the center?" Ethan questioned.

I looked at them. I knew they were all going to wonder why I was so worried when he was right; we had a military-approved counselor working for us. There wasn't any reason I should be worried or upset.

"Mindi, what is going on?" Peggy asked, taking on the tone she had when her motherly side came out.

"Did you talk to him?" Ethan questioned.

"About what?" Trinity asked.

I looked at Ethan and let out the breath I was holding.

"It's not that simple." I sighed.

"What went on between the two of you?" he asked. "I noticed there seemed to be some tension between the two of you."

As I looked around at the concern on all of their faces, I knew I would have to tell them the entire story, so I picked up my drink, took a sip, and then began, telling them everything.

"So, to answer your question, I haven't talked to him because I don't think we'll ever speak again."

"I don't think you need to worry about that. I mean, look at Thomas and I."

"Yeah, we were separated for years, and she wasn't easy to get back when I returned."

"Oh, please."

"Did I tell you that she tried to poison me with chicken and dumplings?" Thomas said, smiling and then winking at Trinity.

"If you aren't careful, I will make that for dinner tomorrow night."

I couldn't help but giggle as everyone laughed and then turned to me.

"Communication, my dear, is key. Give him some time. He is probably struggling with everything. Then take your time and explain things to him. I promise you, it will make a difference," Ethan added.

"Yes, and talk to him about Sarah and the application," Thomas said, reaching over and patting my shoulder.

I looked at them and smiled.

"Thank you for listening. I don't know what I'd do without you guys."

Peggy made her way over to the oven and began pulling out the dishes, setting them on the island.

"That's why you don't have to. Now let's dig in, shall we?" Trinity said, bringing over a stack of plates.

"Yes, let's," I said, grabbing the silverware jar and placing it on the island as well.

Noah

The Week Before Christmas

Dinner with Iris and Zach had been wonderful, and I'd left there with a plan to speak to Mindi this week, only she hadn't been to the community center at all. In fact, she'd called in every day this week, and Sarah hadn't shown up for her appointment either.

It was a little after ten when I left The Crispy Biscuit, coffee in hand. I'd intended to head on over to the bookstore but was surprised when I looked across the street to see Mindi's car in the parking lot, a light dusting of snow covering it.

I glanced both ways and ran across the street to the community center, pulling the door open.

"Hey, Ethan," I said, raising my hand to him as he stood in the hallway helping one kid with his hat.

"Morning, Noah. I wasn't expecting to see you this morning. Did you decide to come and join us for skating time?"

I glanced at my watch and then remembered seeing the memo in my email about that yesterday, but I'd forgotten to reply.

"I actually came in to see Mindi. We kept missing each other this week, and I just saw her car outside."

Ethan glanced over his shoulder at her closed door, finished up with Tyson's hat, and sent him on his way before turning to me.

"You haven't spoken to her yet?"

"No, we sort of had a bit of a falling out, and..."

"Yeah, I know. I could sense the tension between the two of you. So I asked, and she told us the other night at dinner. She was pretty upset. We talked her into speaking with you, and she said she was going to speak with you this week. So, just to make it clear, you haven't spoken to her at all, in any way?"

"No, I uh, I haven't heard from her at all. Today is the first day I think she's been here."

"She didn't email you or call either?" Ethan frowned, once again looking at her door with concern.

"No, not a word. Why, is something wrong?"

Ethan once again glanced at the door and then shook his head.

"I'll leave you to it. I got to go deal with the kids and then pick up the hot chocolate for them."

"Have a good one. I might pop out after."

"Great, hope to see you."

Ethan took off out the door, and that was when Mindi's door opened and she came out of her office, accompanied by two men and a woman who were dressed in military uniforms. She spoke quietly with them and then shook their hands, nodding as they spoke. I watched as they turned and began walking my way, the three of them nodding at me. Once they left the building, I looked back toward Mindi's office, noticing that she was gone.

I made my way to her office door and poked my head inside. She stood with her back to the door, her shoulders shaking as if she were crying.

"Hey," I said, not wanting to startle her.

She turned around and looked at me. Her eyes were darker than I'd ever seen them, which concerned me.

"Hey, Noah," she mumbled before blowing her nose.

"Could we talk?" I asked, my eyes running over her body.

She turned away from me and shook her head. "Right now isn't a great time."

"It won't take long," I promised.

The air between us grew thicker as she stood there and let out a sigh before turning to me.

"Fine, what do you want?" she barked as she looked at me.

"Who were you speaking with?" I questioned.

"It doesn't matter who they were. Now what do you want?" she asked, glaring at me.

"I want to talk to you about the other night," I said.

"There really isn't much to say," she said, flopping down in her chair. "It's done, you said so yourself. So really there is no point in trying to discuss things."

"I know what I said, but I wasn't fair to you. I should have given you a chance to explain, but I didn't. So I'm asking you to tell me your side of things."

There were so many questions in her eyes as she stared at me. "Fine, what do you want to know?"

"I want to know what happened between us," I said.

"Well, according to you, you already know," she said, glaring at me.

I didn't blame her for being so standoffish. I'd been horrible to her after we'd spent a wonderful night together.

"Mindi, please tell me your side."

"What? Why? So you won't believe me again?"

"Please, Mindi."

"Fine, I got that stupid card a few weeks ago. I never

got it the year you sent it. Instead, I got a letter, and I responded, only to have it returned to me. I continued to write to you for an entire year after that, while I waited, holding my breath, for a single response from you. Only I never heard a word. Your parents had left, the military wouldn't answer me, and without knowing if you were alive or dead, it was pointless to continue, so I stopped."

"You stopped?"

"Yes, I stopped writing to you. I had no choice but to assume you were dead, and mourning you was the only way I could get over you and move on."

The room grew quiet as we looked at one another. It was on the tip of my tongue to ask her about the letters in the box I'd seen on her dresser.

"What is it?" she demanded.

"What?"

"What do you want to know? I can see you're teetering on asking me something, so just get it out of the way."

"I saw the letters in the box, next to the Christmas card."

"So that automatically makes you think I've had that card all along, and what, that I just dig those out to torture myself every year? I may not have much of a life, but I do have one."

"Why would you say that? You have an amazing life."

"Listen, I don't need you to tell me how amazing my life is. What you need to know is that when I got that card, I took a trip down memory lane, probably more times than I should have. I hadn't opened them in years."

"Okay, so you say the letters you wrote were returned to you. Where are those letters?"

She looked at me, eyes full of tears and disbelief that I'd ask her that. Without a word, she turned around, opened the door of the cupboard behind her, and reached up, pulling down a black box. She turned back to me, placing the box down on the desk and wiping the lid, removing a thick layer of dust before lifting the lid to see an entire box full of those pink envelopes she used to send me.

"Here," she said, "take it."

I took a step forward as she made her way over toward the window and looked out over the park. I grabbed two of the letters from the box, both marked with a return to sender stamp.

"Mindi, I—"

"Just take them Noah. They are yours, after all. Take them, read them, burn them, do whatever you want; I don't care. Just take them and go." She sniffled.

I stood there, afraid to make a move for fear she got angry or upset. They'd all been returned to her because I'd left the post I'd been stationed at right after Christmas that year. They moved me to an undisclosed location. I couldn't tell anyone where I was going, so it wasn't a wonder that those letters had been returned.

"Mindi, you need to know—"

"I need to know nothing. Now I told you to take them. You got what you wanted."

She spun around, picked up the box, and shoved it toward me. "Get out!" she screamed.

I backed up and out into the hall when she whipped the box in my direction and slammed her office door shut. She pulled the blinds down and left me standing in the hallway with the box of letters.

I stood there, shocked that she'd thrown me out, but yet I waited for a bit, to see if she'd open the door. After a while, I finally gave up and picked up the box on the floor, then left the community center and made my way home.

I pushed my empty plate off to the side and picked up the bottle of beer I'd been nursing during the hockey game. My team had just scored, and yet I didn't feel even the slightest amount of happiness. The confrontation with Mindi this afternoon was weighing heavily on my mind, and then I glanced at the black box I'd brought home. I hadn't had the courage to open it yet, but I'd looked over at it many times tonight.

Finally, I reached over and pulled the lid off the box, pulling out the letter that lay on top. I looked over the envelope. The postmark was almost exactly one year after I'd sent that Christmas card. The envelope was tattered, dirty, but unopened, and so I took a deep breath and opened the letter. There wasn't much written, but what was written was direct and to the point.

Dear Noah,

It's been a year since I last heard from you. While I've tried to get an updated address or location for you, the military is keeping tight-lipped. I'm guessing that perhaps something horrible has happened to you, and while I have tried to keep hope alive that one day you will return, I know I need to move on. I can't keep living in this state of the unknown. So, as hard as it might be, especially at this time of the year, I have to say goodbye to you and the dream of us being together. My heart will forever be yours. Until we meet again, Mindi.

I stared at the words she'd written. She'd been telling me the truth.

I dug into the box and pulled another letter from the center of the box, seeing the same thing on the envelope. The postmark date and then returned. I reached in and pulled another one to see the same thing once again.

Instead of just pulling a random letter, I grabbed the entire pile in the box, every one of them said the same thing.

I'd been an absolute fool.

I flipped the letters over and took the very first one she'd written, opened the envelope, and began reading.

Mindi

My head pounded as I left the community center. It had been a day from hell. The confrontation with Noah was just the icing on an already bad day. I glanced at my watch, noticing the time, and let out a sigh. I'd told Sarah I'd be home over two hours ago, but I had to stay and wait because I'd been so upset. I was just about to climb into the car when my cell phone rang. Grabbing it from my purse, I answered.

"Hello."

"Mindi, are you okay??" I heard Sarah ask.

"Yeah, sweetheart, I'm fine. I got a little sidetracked, so I am going to stop at the Deep Dish and bring home a pizza for dinner."

"Oh, yay!"

"You want your usual?" I questioned.

"Yes, please, maybe with extra pepperoni and cheese."

"You got it. That sounds fantastic. Okay, I will be there shortly. Everything okay?"

"Yeah, I was just getting worried. Gabe and Connor came over and closed up the lot for me."

"Great, okay, I will be home soon."

"Okay, see you soon. Oh, and I put the lights on outside; it looks so pretty. Christmas is my favorite time here."

I smiled to myself as I listened to her, and then the realization of what I had to tell her tonight hit me, making me feel sick to my stomach. Just before Noah had arrived at the community center I'd been told my application for adoption had been denied.

"Great, you can put the tree on too, and I'll see you soon."

"Already done!"

I hung up the phone, my eyes burning with tears as I shoved my phone into my purse. I'd held onto the hope that my application would be good enough after having Sarah live with me for so long. I'd provided her with a stable environment, given her the emotional support she needed, and had even recently gotten her help with Noah. I'd known that everyone in the community I'd placed on my list as a reference had spoken highly of me; however, it hadn't been enough. This would be our last Christmas together, and it was going to break me to have to tell her.

"Mindi, I had an idea for next year with the tree farm," Sarah said, slipping another piece of pizza from the box.

"Oh?" I said, that sick feeling coming back to me once again.

I'd done my best to clear my mind on the drive home, so that I could enjoy one of our last nights together.

"Yeah, I was looking at the stand tonight when I was out helping in the lot, and I thought maybe next year, we could do a permanent hot chocolate station. I mean, I know you bring that in once per season, but I thought it would add something special for people coming on out and getting their tree, especially for those who go out to cut their own."

"Well, it's something to think about. I'd just need to find someone who wouldn't mind manning the part of it."

"Well, I was thinking maybe I could do it. I mean, if that is okay with you. I'd be really careful, and I'd even ask if maybe Brooke and Tristan would allow me to come in and learn how to serve some hot drinks."

I nodded, not sure how I was going to break the news to her that, come New Year's Eve, she'd be leaving my house to move to an entire foster care center.

"Brooke told me it wouldn't be a problem. She'd just put me behind the counter, and I could get hot chocolate from the dispenser when it was ordered. I could work at that and be ready for next season. Please?"

I picked a piece of pepperoni off my slice of pizza and shoved it into my mouth as she sat there, her eyes filled with excitement at the idea and hope I'd say yes.

"Maybe we could even set up a decorate your own Potts Tree Farm ornament. I was looking online, and I found someone who provides clay ornaments you can paint just like the ones we did at the community center this year. Here, let me show you," she said, getting up off the couch and grabbing her tablet.

She sat back down beside me and turned the screen on and began showing me all the things she'd found, excitement filling her voice the more she talked about it. Then she looked over at me, her eyes wide, and wrapped her arms around my neck.

"I love living here, and even though this Christmas isn't over yet, I am so excited for next year. I am going to take a bath before we watch the next movie. Thank you so much for loving me."

I hugged her tight and then let her go, watching her

head on down the hall. I sat there looking around the room. I'd made so many mistakes over the course of the last couple of years. The first one was not being forward with Sarah when she came to live with me about her future with me because somehow I'd always known it would come to this moment. I just wished it would have been the way I'd wanted it.

I leaned back against the couch and listened to the sound of the tub running down the hall. I closed my eyes, trying to figure out how I was going to tell her. I heard the phone ring but didn't move. I wasn't in the mood to talk to anyone at the moment.

I picked up my phone and opened my email, opening the letter that the general I'd met with earlier today had sent, outlining our conversation and all the upcoming information I needed about Sarah.

"Mindi, Ethan is on the phone," Sarah sang, causing me to quickly shut my phone off.

"Oh, thanks. Go have your bath," I said, taking the phone from her and smiling.

Once I heard the bathroom door close, I sat back down and lifted the phone to my ear.

"Hey, Ethan."

"Mindi, what happened today?" he asked.

I let out the breath I was holding. I should have known he'd be calling me about the meeting. After all, he'd been at the center when the three men had arrived. I swallowed hard as I tried to form the words to tell him it didn't go as planned.

"Ethan, I..." The lights on the tree in front of me blurred as tears formed in my eyes.

"What is it?"

"They denied me," I answered, swallowing hard, blinking away the tears.

"I don't understand. What did they say?"

I glanced over my shoulder to make sure Sarah wasn't listening behind me and then took a deep breath.

"They said that while everyone they spoke to gave me nothing but glowing recommendations, they didn't feel that it was a suitable environment. The fact that I am single weighed heavily on their decision."

"Mindi, this makes little sense. You were going to speak with Noah the morning after our holiday dinner. His review and recommendation would have sealed the deal."

I closed my eyes and wiped the tears that ran down my cheeks.

"I know it would have," I whispered.

"What do you mean by that? Did you not speak to Noah and ask him to fill out that portion of the paperwork?"

"Ethan, it really isn't that easy. I wanted to do this on my own."

"My dear, you are a strong individual, independent and self-reliant, and you love to help others. You also need to know when you need to ask for help. Knowing when to ask for that help doesn't show weakness but strength."

"What do you mean?"

"Well, sometimes being so stubborn and not asking for that help shows weakness. It's a fine line, and I think there comes a time and a point when we all learn that. You can't do everything on your own, kid. It's not a weakness to ask for help."

"I know," I muttered.

I heard the bathroom door open down the hall and Sarah humming along to a Christmas song.

"I'll be right there, Mindi!" she yelled from the hallway.

"Okay, sweetie," I called.

"I know you have to go, but let me ask you, have you told her yet?" Ethan asked.

"I haven't, but I will within the next couple of days."

"Okay. I will let you go, and I am sorry it's come down to this. I will see you at the center in a couple of days for Santa."

"Me too, and I will see you then."

I hung up the phone just as Sarah came into the room dressed in the new Christmas pajamas I'd just gotten her a couple of weeks ago. She sat down on the couch, grabbed a blanket, and smiled at me.

"Can we watch *The Grinch* again?"

I smiled. "Sure can. Want some popcorn?"

"Can we add some of those candy-covered chocolates?"

"Sure can. Come on, let's go get that snack, and then we will curl up and watch the movie." I winked.

Noah

It was a frosty morning. A fresh blanket of snow covered the ground. I'd spent the entire night reading Mindi's letters, and I could see how with each letter, her hope that I'd return was diminishing, as had mine when I never heard from her.

Now that I knew the truth, I planned to speak with her before the children arrived to give Santa their final wish list before Christmas.

As I made my way down the street, I passed by Bluebird Books and stopped in. The front windows of the store displayed lights, Christmas decorations, and as many Christmas books as Trinity could put in them.

I pulled the door open and stepped inside, the floor giving away that same creak it had when I was a boy. The place hadn't changed much, just expanded, and it still smelled the same. I'd always sworn they pumped the smell of ink and paper in the air when I was younger. Now I was almost certain of it. Peggy and Trinity sat at the counter, Christmas music playing, having a coffee.

"Morning, Noah," Trinity greeted.

"Morning, ladies," I said, heading over to the fiction section.

"Need help finding anything?" Trinity questioned.

"Nah, I'm good," I said. "Enjoy your coffee." I winked and went about looking through the titles. I eventually went into the other room and continued looking for something to read as the store got busier. I was going through the new fiction releases when I heard a woman talking on the other side of the shelf. I did my best to ignore it, but when I heard Mindi's name, I had no choice but to listen.

"So she was wrong all along."

"Yes, she was, Noah never died. In fact, he is in the other room," I heard Trinity say.

As much as I wanted to poke my head around the corner to see who they were speaking to, I decided against it.

"So what Diana told me was true, that Fred delivered a lost card to her a couple of weeks ago? Apparently, it was a Christmas card from ten years ago, and inside there was a proposal. Now, do you know if it's true that they have started seeing one another?"

"LuAnn, how did you get hold of this information?" I heard Peggy ask.

"It's the talk all over town. I miss one tree lighting in all my years in Willow Valley and something like this happens. It's headline news."

"Care to tell us who your source is?" Trinity questioned.

"I won't. I knew I should have gone. I was feeling under the weather and had no choice but to stay in bed. Anyway, I have heard through the grapevine that things apparently didn't go very well. Word has it that Noah found the card at her place and all hell broke loose. I stopped in at the community center to do an article on the upcoming Christmas events, but Mindi wasn't her usual self and refused to speak with me."

"Oh?"

"She was so closed-off to communication, instead I interviewed Ethan about the article. He claimed she wasn't feeling well and had to go home. Personally, I think he was lying to me."

"LuAnn, I'd like to remind you who you are talking to," I heard Peggy say.

"I'm sorry, dear, but it's true. You know, I think she has just gone over the edge with all this. I think she is still in love with him, and now all this with Sarah."

"All what with Sarah?" Trinity asked.

"I'll tell you later," Peggy mumbled.

I leaned around the corner and looked over at the three women standing at the counter with a frown on my face, wondering what was going on with Sarah.

"Didn't you hear? Mindi was denied in the adoption process."

"What?"

I could see the shock on Trinity's face.

"Where did you hear that?" Peggy questioned.

"Again, I won't out my source. I feel bad for her. All I know is that all eyes are on her right now. She is literally the talk of the town. People who've never gone to Potts Tree Farm have gone out there in the hope of catching a glimpse of her."

"LuAnn, if you feel bad for her, then why would you want to approach her for an article?"

Finally, they were sticking up for her, I thought to myself as I waited to hear this woman's answer.

"Well, at first, I wasn't contacting her for an article, but now that I know the adoption wasn't approved because Noah didn't fill out the paperwork, I want his contact information. *The Gazette* has asked me to do an article on the soldier who returned from the dead. They want to know if he has done this to get back at her."

"I see."

Peggy looked at Trinity and then turned away from the women at the counter.

"LuAnn, I don't think any of this is any of the town's business."

"Well, I do. You know that news never sleeps. Well, unless one is ill."

I wasn't waiting for Trinity or Peggy to say another word. Instead, I stepped out from the other room and cleared my throat, watching as LuAnn glanced at me over her shoulder.

"I couldn't help but overhear you're looking to do an article on the soldier who returned from the dead?" I questioned.

"Why yes, I am. Do you know him?" she questioned.

"Sure do."

"Wonderful, tell me where I can find him?"

I chuckled and stepped forward a little more, coming up beside her. I put my arm around her and leaned in. "I'm him, and you can tell *The Gazette*, it's a no-go."

I placed the book I was going to buy on the counter and walked out of the store without a word to anyone.

I felt like my heart was going to beat out of my chest at what LuAnn had said. I hadn't filled out paperwork for Mindi? What was that about? I didn't know I was supposed to fill anything out. Confusion filled me now as I made my way over to the center.

My heart was pounding as I made my way into the community center. I ran to Mindi's office, but her door and blinds were closed. I was about to knock when I heard my name. I turned to see Ethan round the corner.

"Hey, Noah, glad you are here. I need some help in the auditorium to fix the tree before Santa gets here."

"Oh, I wanted to speak with Mindi."

"She is in there with Sarah. She should be done shortly. Can you give me a hand first?"

I looked back at her door and then nodded, following Ethan into the auditorium where we got to work on the tree. Somehow, someone had bumped into it, knocking the fake tree crooked, and while Ethan climbed up on the ladder, I held the base of the tree, hoping we could straighten it without having to take anything off it. A couple of quick twists, and we were able to fix it.

Ethan came down off the ladder, while I straightened up the Santa chair. It was then we heard a door slam and saw Sarah run off past the auditorium door.

"What was that all about?" I questioned, looking at Ethan.

Ethan looked over at me, and then looked over at the

doorway where Mindi stood, her eyes red, tears streaming down her face. She barely even took notice of my being there; instead, she ran over to Ethan and collapsed against him, sobbing into his chest.

"Oh, sweetheart," he soothed, wrapping his arms around her.

"I broke her heart," she sobbed.

Ethan rested his head on top of hers as she sobbed against him. I looked over at the door, wondering where Sarah had gone, and decided I'd go over and speak with her, leaving Ethan with Mindi.

I walked down the hall and stopped when I passed my office. The room was dark, but I could hear a tiny cry coming from within. I walked over and flipped the light on to see Sarah curled up on my couch crying.

"Hey, kiddo. What's going on?" I questioned, making my way over to sit beside her.

She continued to cry, and then sat up and wrapped her arms around my neck.

"I thought I'd be with Mindi forever, but she just told me I have to leave."

"I see."

"The military is taking me to a foster home on New Year's Eve. I don't want to go," she sobbed. "Mindi is my best friend, and she created a home for me when I was hurting."

"I'm sorry, sweetheart. Sometimes the military doesn't look at those things. They look at what is best for you."

She looked at me, her blue eyes now bloodshot and puffy from crying.

"I don't understand. They don't care that she has given me a safe and loving home?"

"I don't know. I haven't spoken to them to know what their reasons are."

"Do you think Mindi doesn't want me?" She sniffled.

My heart broke as I looked down at her, because I knew for a fact that Mindi loved having Sarah with her. That was one thing I was certain of. I took a moment, and then I cleared my throat.

"Sarah, I don't think that at all."

She nodded, and then rested her head against my chest.

"Do you think if I ask Santa really nicely, he will give me my Christmas wish?"

I didn't know what to tell her. There was no way I could say yes to that question. Instead, I took a deep breath and whispered, "You can always ask, no harm in that."

Mindi left the community center with Sarah shortly after all the kids had seen Santa. Ethan and I remained to clean some things up, and once we were finished, we both locked up the door.

"What are your plans for tonight?" Ethan asked.

I looked at him and shrugged my shoulders. "I think I might go out and speak with Mindi."

"I wouldn't. I think she just needs to spend some time with Sarah," Ethan said.

I took a deep breath and then looked at him. "Ethan, do you know anything about the whole situation with Sarah?"

"I do."

"I was in the bookstore earlier today, and there was this woman LuAnn..."

Ethan chuckled. "Good old LuAnn," he said, shaking his head.

"What does that mean?"

"Exactly what I said. LuAnn is somewhat of a gossip. She says a lot of things that are rather hurtful and that shouldn't be said. What gossip is she spreading now?"

I looked over at the skating rink where a few boys played hockey, and then looked back at Ethan.

"She mentioned something about the Sarah situation and said it was my fault. Something about paperwork."

Ethan averted his eyes from me and grew quiet for a

moment. "I really shouldn't be telling you any of this, but, if you have time for a coffee, I will fill you in."

I glanced at my watch, already knowing I had nowhere to be. "Let's go."

Together, we left the community center parking lot and made our way over to The Crispy Biscuit where we shared a bite to eat and a coffee, and I listened with open ears to Ethan tell me the entire story.

Mindi

December 30

I walked up the front steps of the porch and opened the door, stepping into the warm house. Snow had been falling since I'd started cleaning up the tree lot this morning. I kicked my boots off and shrugged out of my coat, making my way into the living room where Sarah sat on the couch, her books in front of her, trying to decide which ones to take and which to donate.

"Want some hot chocolate?" I asked, warming my hands by the fire.

"No." She sighed, a sad look on her face.

"Are you sure? I'm going to add those little snowman marshmallows."

"Yeah, I'm sure. I won't be able to have those things anymore, so I figure I may as well stop having them now."

Sarah hadn't been herself ever since I'd told her she'd be leaving. When she found out that she was the recipient of the town's donations this year, she thanked everyone and then insisted that I donate everything to the less fortunate. Even the things I'd gotten her for Christmas hadn't put a smile on her face, which had broken my heart.

"Oh, there is a message there for you. I forgot the name of the person who called, but I wrote the number down on the paper there."

"Ah, okay."

I picked up the paper and made my way into the kitchen, putting the kettle on while I dialed the number on the paper. While the phone rang, I heard a knock at the front door and glanced out into the living room at Sarah.

"Can you get that?" I questioned.

Sarah nodded, getting up from where she was sitting.

"Hello, Sergeant Gardner's office. How can I help you?" a woman's voice said on the other end of the phone.

My stomach flipped the moment I heard whose office it was. I swallowed hard, wondering if they were sending someone early to pick up Sarah.

"Hello, this is Mindi Potts. Someone called for me."

"Oh yes, Mindi, one moment. Sergeant Gardner wanted to speak with you before he left today."

While I waited for the kettle to boil, I reached up and poured a handful of marshmallows into my cup, when I heard a man's voice in the living room. I listened a little harder while I waited for the sergeant to pick up and was almost sure I heard Noah in the living room.

"Mindi, thank you for calling me back," I heard the sergeant say, who only days ago ripped my heart from my chest when he told me they had denied my application.

"No problem. Sorry, I was outside when you called earlier."

"No problem. Listen, I wanted to talk to you about Sarah."

"Look, before you start, I am going to ask that you leave her with me until the agreed-upon pickup date. She is struggling, and I am trying my hardest to get her to be okay with the situation."

"Mindi, please let me speak."

"Okay," I said, knowing full well that if they wanted to come and pick her up now, then that was how it was to be; there wasn't any room to argue with them.

"Mindi, we have reconsidered your application, and I am pleased to tell you that Sarah will not be leaving Willow Valley. We are granting your request."

I felt my heart skip a beat as the words he'd spoken sunk in. I swallowed hard, my body heating with excitement.

"Are you serious?"

"I am. You see, when the last part of the application came through over the holidays, we all agreed that Sarah would be best suited with you, and that moving her would only hinder her healing."

I frowned at his words. What last part of the application, I wondered to myself.

"So, if you are ready to accept the responsibility of raising Sarah, the job is yours."

"While I am thrilled with this news, may I ask what you received?"

"Yes, of course. Apparently, the last part of the application, the therapist's report, somehow got lost with the original fax that was sent in, it came in on Christmas Eve and was waiting for me when I returned to my office on the twenty-seventh. I immediately took it to the team, and they got back to me today, so I wanted to call before much longer to give you the news. Congratulations, and I hope you and Sarah enjoy your New Year together."

"We will, thank you," I replied, hanging up the phone.

I took a moment to digest the news, leaning against the counter, tears rolling down my cheeks as I released all the tension I'd felt since hearing their first decision.

Once I calmed down, I took a sip of my hot chocolate and made my way into the living room to see Sarah sitting with Noah, talking and laughing. They both looked my way, waiting for me to speak.

"Look who came over," Sarah said, breaking the silence, a smile on her face for the first time in days.

"I see that."

"Who called?" Sarah questioned.

"It was Sergeant Gardner."

I looked over at Sarah to see the smile immediately vanish from her face.

"What did he want?"

"He called to tell me that..." I swallowed hard, overcome with emotion once again.

"To tell you what?" Sarah questioned, crossing her arms. "I'm not leaving early, am I?"

"You aren't leaving at all," I said, swallowing hard.

"What?" she said, lifting her eyes to me.

"I....you are staying with me. They changed their minds."

Sarah immediately jumped up off the couch and came running to me, wrapping her arms around me tight.

"Santa answered my wish," she cried.

I hugged her to me, not wanting to let go for fear this might be a dream. When we finally parted, Sarah grabbed her box of books and looked at both Noah and me.

"I'm off to put these back on my shelf. Can I put my Christmas lights back up too?" she asked with excitement.

"Absolutely, they are in the box at the end of the hall."

"I know where they are," she said, running out of the room.

After Sarah had been gone a few moments, I looked over at Noah, who sat there watching me.

"You didn't have to do—"

"I didn't have to, but I did. Don't get angry, but Ethan told me everything. I wasn't going to interfere, but I saw how unhappy you both were, and it broke me. Why didn't you just ask me?"

It was that then the tears poured.

"I thought you hated me. I didn't think you'd do anything for me after the other day, so I didn't bother to ask."

"Mindi, I read your letters."

I looked at him, shocked. "You did?"

"I did. All of those letters were sent to the old base. They transferred me to a new base shortly after Christmas that year. It was a top-secret location, which was why you couldn't get the information. I'd forgotten about that until I saw the address on the envelopes."

"I don't know what to say."

"You don't need to say anything. You've been through enough pain, and I couldn't stand to see something else taken something from you. That was why I stepped up and sent in the paperwork. I wanted to see you smile again because, after reading your letters, I realized that you probably haven't truly smiled in a long time. I also realized the life I missed out on with you. I don't want to waste any more time."

"You don't?"

"I don't. I want to work through everything with you and move on from here. Start over, and start new."

Tears once again flooded my eyes as I looked at him. My throat was so tight, yet I still got out a thank you before he got up from where he sat and wrapped me in his arms.

As I turned off the lights in the living room and made my way down the hall where I stopped outside of Sarah's door. I pushed it open a little and poked my head in to see Sarah sound asleep under the glow of Christmas lights.

I leaned against the door, watching her, smiling to myself as I realized that Brooke had been right. Willow Valley was magical at Christmas. Sarah was staying, and for that I was forever grateful. Noah had returned, and even though things didn't go as I'd always imagined they would, we had a new beginning ahead of us.

GET A FREE BOOK

Sign up for my newsletter and I'll send you a free book.

https://geni.us/NLSignupBackMatter

What is coming next from S.L. Sterling

To see what is coming next from me visit my website where you can always see the list of upcoming titles that are currently available for preorder.

https://geni.us/ComingSoonfromSterling

Follow S.L. Sterling

Did you know that bookbub has a feature where you can follow me and it will send you an alert when I release a book or put a title on sale? Sign up here and make sure you stay in the loop.

Bookbub:
https://geni.us/SLSterlingBookbub

Website
https://www.authorslsterling.com

Facebook
https://geni.us/SLSterlingFB

Twitter
https://geni.us/SLSterlingTwitter

Instagram
https://geni.us/SLSterlingInstagram

Tiktok
https://geni.us/slsterlingtiktok

Reader Group

https://geni.us/SapphiresReaderGroup

Goodreads
https://geni.us/SterlingGoodreads

Newsletter
https://geni.us/NLSignupBackMatter

An avid reader all her life, S.L. Sterling dreamt of becoming an author. She decided to give writing a try after one of her favorite authors launched a course on how to write your novel. This course gave her the push she needed to put pen to paper and her debut novel "It Was Always You" was born.

When S.L. Sterling isn't writing or plotting her next novel she can be found curled up with a cup of coffee, blanket and the newest romance novel from one of her favorite authors.

In her spare time, she enjoys camping, hiking, sunny destinations, spending quality time with family and friends and of course reading.

To be notified of new releases or sales, join S.L. Sterling's private Mailing List.
https://geni.us/NLSignupBackMatter

Get even more of the inside scoop when you join S.L. Sterling's private Facebook group, Sterling's Silver Sapphires: https://geni.us/SapphiresReaderGroup

His to Hold

Finding Forever with You

Vegas MMA

Dagger

The Doctors of Eastport

Doctor Desire

Doctor Right

Doctor Frost

All I Want for Christmas (Contemporary Romance Holiday
Collection)

The Happy Holidates Collection

Pop Tarts and Mistletoe

Champagne and Fireworks

Summer Nights and Fireflies

Vancouver Dominators

Inside the Penalty Box

Ten Minute Misconduct

Crossing the Red Line

Two Minutes for Holding

Playing the Neutral Zone

Through the Five Hole

Willow Valley

Memories of the Past

The Holiday Dilemma

Letters from the Heart

My Darling Christmas

Scars on my Heart

Returning to Me